SOUL SURVIVOR

LARA'S STORY

I would rather die a meaningful death than to live a meaningless life.
Corazon Aquino

Let me embrace thee, sour adversity, for wise men say it is the wisest course.
William Shakespeare

BY

G S WILLMOTT

CONTENTS

AUTHOR'S PREVIOUS TITLES

The Other Side of the Trench – The Spirit of War

Brothers in Arms

Escape – True Accounts of POW Escapes

Red Lights on the Somme

You Forgot the Sauce – An Alzheimer's Journey You Won't Forget

Survival – An Americans Family's Odyssey Through Two World Wars

Boy's Own War – Boy Warriors Fighting Through the Ages

ACKNOWLEDGEMENTS

Anna for being my wife.

Sheelagh Wedgeman For a great edit

Desma Paccito For another fantastic cover

Ian Irvine For input on the music scene of the mid to late sixties

Preview Readers:

Kim Krarup

Jane Sexton

Rebekah Grubb

Ian Jones

David Needum

Cenred Harmsworth

DISASTER

CHAPTER 1

Intrepid

July 1948

Jack and Anna had been planning the family holiday at Chesapeake since war's end when they discovered the entire family had survived the horrors of the shocking conflict in Europe and the Pacific.

Julie and Harry were taking time off from their medical practice in London and flying to New York then on to Washington. From there they would meet Tom and Peter and drive to Chesapeake. They decided to leave Lara with her nanny as they felt the trip would be too arduous.

Lucy, the matriarch of the family, was now seventy-one yet quite active, and had been living at the Chesapeake beach house since the death of her husband, Gene.

On 3rd July the family all arrived at the house; it was the first time in years that the clan had got together for a holiday.

At six that evening Anna summoned everybody to meet in the summer room overlooking the bay. She asked Peter to pop the corks on two bottles of 1928 vintage *Krug*. Joe, her first husband, had been storing it in the wine cellar below the house for many years.

'I would like everybody to charge their glasses. Here's to the Doherty family – long may we live.'

'Hear, hear!' They all raised their glasses.

'Mother, this Champagne is magnificent where on earth did you find it?' asked Tom.

'My little secret darling. But I can tell you there's more where that came from.'

Jack rose and proposed another toast.

'Here's to my father Joe and my stepfather Gene – may they both rest in peace.'

'Thank you, darling.' His mother smiled.

After the toasts were over, they moved into the dining room where Sarah, the maid had set a beautiful table.

The meal was excellent and included seafood and roast loin of lamb. The wine was Californian.

'Well everybody, it wasn't too long ago that I was sitting in the dust with my bowl and a handful of rice. When I was marched through the gates of River Valley Road Camp my weight was one hundred and eighty pounds. When I was liberated I was down to ninety pounds and here I am with the people I love most in the world eating fine food and drinking excellent wine. I thank God I am alive. By the way, I now weigh one hundred and seventy pounds.' Tom had a tear in his eye.

'A toast to Tom.' Lucy held her glass up, and everybody followed her lead.

'Unfortunately, Julie and I can tell a very similar story to Tom's. All we would like to say is we are very happy to be with you all. And alive.' Harry said.

'May I suggest we retire to the lounge room? I have another surprise for you all.'

The family did as requested. Waiting for them were brandy balloons and a very impressive bottle of cognac.

Tom announced, 'This bottle of cognac has been in our cellar for as long as I remember, unopened. It is Louis XIII. I quote Louis XIII's cellarmaster Pierrette Trichet who said, as he held a crystal glass filled with amber liquid, "It's one century in a glass. The idea is to be very humble in front of this glass and pay respect because it represents the effort and the know-how of one century."'

'Peter, may I ask you to pour a glass for each of us please?'

'Certainly, Mother.'

'Tomorrow I have arranged to take the launch out on the bay. We'll enjoy our 4th of July lunch cruising. I have asked Joe Wilcox to act as skipper so we can enjoy ourselves without worrying about steering the boat, as it were.'

Gradually the family retired to their bedrooms except for Peter and Tom.

'How are your legs holding up, Pete?'

'Yeah, they're OK. I get pain when it gets cold.'

'You'd better move to California then.'

'That's not such a bad idea, Tom. I'm seriously thinking of doing just that.'

'Really?'

'Yeah, I'm thinking of leaving the Marines and enrolling at Stanford. I want to do a post-grad in neurosurgery.'

'Wow, that's a big one. Why neurosurgery?'

'I saw many head wounds in the war. I felt helpless not being able to help the poor bastards. I also look at Julie and Harry and the fantastic work they're doing changing people's lives. I'd like to make a similar contribution.'

'Good on you Pete, I think it's great.'

'So how goes it with you, Tom?'

'It's been hard. I suffered like you wouldn't believe under the Japs. When I was fighting, it all seemed worthwhile. You were doing something for your pals and your country. Once captured, you felt worthless, a failure somehow.'

Tom opened up and recounted the hell ships and his survival of the A-Bombe at Nagasaki.

Peter was aghast.

'I knew it must have been hell, but I had no idea.'

'Yeah, it was fucking horrible. Don't tell Mum – it would distress her too much.'

'OK.'

They hugged each other and retired for the night.

4 July 1948

The Dohertys had breakfast together in the summer room: Pancakes with strawberries, blueberries and vanilla ice cream; red white and blue to honour the day.

The men each took a bottle of wine while the women carried the food, which was to be their Independence Day lunch.

Once boarded, the skipper asked the Doherty men to cast off the ropes, and they were under way. The weather was perfect, blue skies with the odd puffy white cloud. The only negative was that the wind had picked up and was quite strong. Inclement weather was of no concern to the *Intrepid*; she was 100 feet long and powered by an 800 horsepower diesel engine.

About an hour out from the shore the women started to prepare the lunch in the galley while the men were on deck talking, smoking and enjoying themselves.

At 1p.m. Julie called the boys down to have their lunch. Harry had just lit a large Cuban cigar and was annoyed that he had to throw it over the side; however he did as he was told.

The group including Joe, the skipper, were seated at the yacht's dining table and presented with various dishes, all decorated with the stars and stripes.

'Well, who'd have thought this could happen just eighteen months ago, sitting down to a fabulous Fourth of July lunch on a luxury yacht in the middle of Chesapeake Bay', said Tom.

Peter agreed. 'We've all very lucky considering what we've all been through.'

'I smell smoke. Can anybody else smell it?' asked Julie.

'It's probably the smoke from Harry's cigar still lingering about,' replied Pete. 'Bloody cigars – they'll kill you one day, Harry.'

'No, it's not cigar smoke. I quite like the smell of a fine cigar,' commented Julie.

'The hot plates aren't on, are they Mum?'

'No, I haven't used them today. We cooked up at the house.'

'Look! There's smoke coming in under the galley door. There must be a fire up on deck.' Joe's voice sounded panicked.

'You ladies stay down here, and we'll check out what's happening!' instructed Pete.

'Shit, the door's locked! No, that's impossible. Must be jammed.'

The four men tried to push the door open, but it wouldn't budge. They grabbed the fire extinguisher and began bashing the door with the heavy cylinder. Not what it was designed for in the case of a fire. The galley was filling with smoke and everybody started coughing uncontrollably. They tried bashing the portholes with the fire extinguisher, but it made no impact. Harry told the women to lie on the floor below the smoke cloud although that seemed to make no difference. The heat from the fire became intense, singeing the hairs on the men's arms.

What Harry or any of the others hadn't realised was that the cigar had blown back onto the rear deck. It landed on a loosely coiled rope and began to smoulder. The wind and the cruiser's movement fanned the small fire and within a few minutes it had become a major outbreak. Unfortunately, the blaze was located over the reserve fuel tank setting off an explosion that could be heard miles away. *Intrepid* burned furiously and within thirty minutes was a smouldering wreck barely above the waterline.

All aboard perished.

The Dohertys had survived the war, POW camps and the *Titanic*. Now they were gone, apart from Lara.

POOR LITTLE RICH GIRL

CHAPTER 2

1948

Don Bradman scores 201 in 272 minutes versus India

Executive order ending racial segregation in US Armed Forces

Mahatma Gandhi assassinated

July 6 1948

Westmoreland Manor Somerset England

Lisbeth Forsyth was an experienced nanny who had cared for many children of the British aristocracy over the years. She was only twenty-six, and although attractive and quite vivacious she was unmarried. Being a nanny was what she wanted to be, even at high school and she wasn't about to let a love interest get in the way.

Sometimes when she was alone in her room, she felt lonely, but that feeling of loneliness soon disappeared when she saw her children.

Lisbeth had been Lara de Neville's nanny from the time her parents Julie and Harry brought her home from the hospital. Lara was now a happy, healthy six-year-old. She was a very pretty girl with long blonde hair, which she usually wore in plaits. Lisbeth was always delighted when she heard Lara's infectious laugh, which was quite often.

Lisbeth and Lara were playing on the front lawn of Westmoreland Manor, the family home, when they saw a black Rolls Royce approach along the long driveway.

'Who's that Nanny?'

'I don't know, darling. Judging by his car I think he's somebody important. Why don't we go and meet him.'

'OK.'

The car pulled up under the grand portico. A man with white hair, and a dark pin-striped suit alighted from the back of the vehicle.

'Good morning. My name is Sir Horace Winterbottom. I'm the solicitor for the de Neville family. I take it you must be Lisbeth Forsyth?'

'I am. And this is Lara de Neville.'

'I'm pleased to meet you both. I was wondering if we could have a private word, Miss Forsyth?'

'Yes, come into the house. We can speak in the library. Lara, why don't you run into the kitchen and ask Mrs Potter if you can have a glass of milk, and a biscuit.'

Lara skipped off to the kitchen. Lisbeth ushered Sir Horace into the magnificent library and closed the large oak door.

'I'm afraid I have some very disturbing news, Miss Forsyth.'

The solicitor recounted what had happened on the Chesapeake Bay. Lisbeth was dumbfounded. She couldn't believe the whole family had perished.

'I can't believe it. The Earl and Countess were like family to me and what's to become of little Lara?'

The distraught woman couldn't contain her grief and began to sob. Mr Winterbottom waited patiently before continuing.

'What this means Miss Forsyth, is that young Lara has no legal guardian.'

'So what happens now?'

'Well, if you are agreeable I'd like you to care for Lara until a decision is made about her immediate future. Mr Bryant will still run the estate – he's been the caretaker here for many years, so I'm led to believe. The remainder of the staff will remain employed here. I think it's important that Lara is surrounded by people she's familiar with.'

'Who's going to break the news to Lara?'

'I was hoping you would assist me. Naturally, we have to be very compassionate with her. You being present would be a comfort, I'm sure.'

'So do you want to tell her now?'

'I think that would be best, don't you?'

'Yes, I suppose so. I'm not looking forward to it I can tell you.'

'Neither am I.'

'I'll go and fetch her.'

'If you could please, Miss Forsyth.'

Lisbeth approached the kitchen where Lara was enjoying a glass of milk and chatting to the kitchen staff.

'Lara darling, could I ask you to come with me please.'

'Nanny I haven't finished my milk yet, and Miss Lucy was telling me a funny story about her milking a cow.'

'I'm sorry, but it's important. You can finish your milk later.'

'Oh, all right.'

Lara followed behind her nanny until they reached the library. Upon entering she saw Sir Horace standing in front of the fireplace.

'Hello, Lara you can call me Sir Horace. Why don't you sit next to your nanny on the sofa. We've got something to tell you.'

'Is it a story? I love stories.'

'No, I'm afraid it's not a story. It's about your mummy and daddy.'

'They're in America, but they'll be home soon. I do miss them.'

'Lara, I'm afraid Mummy and Daddy won't be coming home. They both had a terrible accident,' said Lisbeth.

'No, they promised me they'd be home soon.'

'Lara you know when we were playing in the garden today we found a little bird that had died?'

'Yes, that was sad.'

'Well Mummy and Daddy died in the accident just like that little bird. They've both gone to heaven.'

'No, no! You're lying! I don't believe you.'

Lara jumped up from the sofa running out of the library and into the garden. Eventually, she stopped running and lay on the grass continuing to cry uncontrollably.

Lisbeth found the distraught little girl and sat next to her on the lawn she placed Lara's head in her lap and consoled her.

'It will be all right, darling. I'm here for you and Mummy and Daddy will always be watching over you. I know it's hard to understand why God took them but he must have had a very special job He wanted them to do.'

'I don't care! I need them here with me. They promised me they'd be home soon. It's not fair.'

Sir Horace decided to take his leave. He intended to speak with Lisbeth the following week about Lara's future, and indeed her own. The solicitor had a reputation for being an insensitive lawyer but as he was driven out of the estate he felt quite sad for little Lara. He knew he would be partly responsible for her upbringing; he intended that she be given every opportunity in life.

Lara's father was the Earl of Westmoreland and Julie, her mother, was an American doctor who married Harry (who was also a doctor) in 1929.

Julie's maiden name was Doherty, a well-known naval family in the United States. Captain Joe Doherty, her father, was lost at sea on the *Titanic* in April 2012. Jack, her brother, graduated from West Point as a naval officer and served in the World War I where he was wounded.

During a long naval career, Jack was promoted several times including being appointed as a senior military officer attached to the American Embassy in Berlin before World War II.

Julie and Jack's stepfather was Rear-Admiral Eugene Leutze.

All of Julie's immediate family, including her mother, died in the explosion on Chesapeake Bay.

Harry's parents, the Earl of Westmoreland and the Countess of Westmoreland died in a train crash when they were travelling to stay at the family's estate Raby Castle, in Scotland.

Raby Castle

A SAD DAY IN JULY

CHAPTER 3

London July 12

The memorial service was organised by the trust members with the assistance of several peers and friends of the couple. Harry, being an Earl, and Julie, being a Countess entitled them to the privilege of a service at Westminster Abbey.

It was held on 12 July with 300 mourners attending including the Prime Minister, Clement Attlee, several members of the House of Lords and members of the couple's golf club, Burnham & Berrow. They were joined by many other friends and work colleagues.

Harry and Julie were both incarcerated in Changi Prison in Singapore during World War II. Several of their fellow prisoners attended the service.

One of the ex-Prisoners of War, Charlie Baker asked if he could speak.

'The Earl and Countess de Neville, Harry and Julie, were an amazing couple; both doctors, both specialising in plastic surgery. Not to alter the nose shape of an actor or actress, but to help give our war veterans a new life by reshaping their faces and bodies after having had horrendous injuries inflicted on them during two world wars. I should know, I was one of them.

'They could have had the good life in Britain, living in magnificent homes and being part of the social scene in London. They chose another direction, living in Singapore on the other side of the globe caring for our troops and their families.

'With the fall off Singapore they were imprisoned in Changi suffering under the cruel rule of the Japanese. They both survived this horrendous chapter in our history only to die with their family in a tragic boating accident.

'We will never forget them.'

Harry and Julie would have been placed in the family mausoleum at Brompton Cemetery if their remains had been recovered however, no remains were ever found. A plaque instead was placed there in memory.

Memorial Service Westminster Abbey

Arlington July 12

Halfway across the world another memorial service was being held on the same day at Arlington National Cemetery for Tom, Peter, and Lucy who were all were part of the Doherty family, a family with a strong military background. More than two hundred mourners attended the service with a large contingent of military officers present.

Let Them Rest in Peace.

Arlington Cemetery

IN GOD WE TRUST

CHAPTER 4

July 14 1948

Lisbeth woke at 6 am. She lay in her bed going over in her mind the questions she would put to Sir Horace; she knew the answers he gave would determine her decision. Putting on her dressing gown, she headed for the bathroom down the hall. Once dressed and made up she quietly climbed the ornate staircase leading to Lara's bedroom. Lisbeth waited at the door to determine if Lara was awake, she heard no sound. Deciding to allow the little girl to sleep for a while longer, the nanny descended the stairs and walked to the large kitchen where the cook, Mrs Potter, was preparing breakfast.

'Good morning Lucy, may I ask you to pour me a cup of tea please?'

'Good morning Miss Forsyth. Yes, certainly I'll bring it into the drawing room if you like.'

'No Lucy, I'll drink it here.'

'Yes, ma'am.'

The young cook made the tea and brought it over to Lisbeth, who was seated at the long oak table where the staff ate their meals.

'Tell me Lucy, are you happy working at Westmoreland?'

'Oh yes, Miss Forsyth. Although I know things will be different without the Earl and Duchess being here. It's so sad to lose them. I can't imagine what it will be like for poor Lara.'

They both heard a noise. It was Lara, standing at the entrance to the kitchen with her teddy bear under her arm.

'Hello darling. Would you like a glass of warm milk?' asked Lucy.

'Yes please.'

'How did you sleep?' asked Lisbeth.

'Not very well. I had a terrible nightmare. I dreamt Mummy and Daddy died.'

'Lara, come here darling.'

The little six-year-old walked slowly over to her nanny and sat beside her at the table.

'Lara it wasn't a nightmare sweetie. Mummy and Daddy have gone to heaven.'

'Why? I don't understand. They promised me they'd be back home soon. Daddy promised he'd buy me a pony when he got back.'

'I'm sorry Lara, but God wanted your mummy and Daddy to be with him. They're very special, and he needed their help to do his work.'

'Will they always be looking down on me?'

'They will be, always, darling.'

'Who's going to look after me?'

'I am, together with all the people in this house. You are a very special girl.'

Lisbeth took the little girl's hand; they made their way to Lara's bathroom. The nanny ran a warm bath in which the little girl soaked for a good half an hour. Lisbeth knew it would be some time before Lara could cope with the everyday life of a six-year-old orphaned girl.

The family solicitor was on time. Lisbeth invited him into the study.

'How is she coping?'

'She's having trouble believing her parents won't be returning, a natural reaction I would have thought.'

'Yes, I'm sure it will be some time before she comes to grips with it.'

'The most important thing is she receives support from us all.'

'I agree, that brings me to the structure of the Trust and most importantly your role in Lara's upbringing. I have spoken to the other members of the trust regarding fostering young Lara.'

'You haven't told me who the Trust members are yet, Sir Horace.'

'Sorry, I should let you know before we continue. There's me of course plus Mr Arnold Harmsworth the family accountant and financial advisor. Mrs Elinor Humphries, Headmistress at St Leonards Preparatory School where Lara is enrolled. Finally, we have been able to find Lara's second cousin Lord Andrew de Neville, the only other surviving member of the family. He also has agreed to become a Trust member.

'So, we all agree Lara needs to have some stability in her life and bringing in strangers to foster her, we believe, would not help with her development, nor her mental state. It is with this in mind that we ask you to consider being her legal guardian.

'The courts would have to approve your appointment, and the Trust will still have the ultimate decision-making power, but it places you in a much stronger position to raise little Lara.'

'Well, I think I'm flattered.

'The only other issue we need to finalise is your appointment as Lara's guardian. I believe your current salary is 100 pounds plus full board, and lodging is that correct?'

'Yes, that's correct.'

'The Trust has agreed, because of your increased responsibility, to increase your annual salary to 500 pounds. We would also expect you to sleep on the same level as Lara, taking one of the bedroom suites close to hers. You will, of course, have access to the estate's motor vehicle and driver and will be the most senior staff member with total access to the manor and its grounds.'

'That's a very generous offer Sir Horace. How many weeks holiday should I expect?'

'Two weeks.'

'I would like some time to consider it. May I suggest I get back to you tomorrow with my answer?'

'Yes, of course, take more time if you need it.'

'I'm sure tomorrow will be all right.'

The meeting concluded, Sir Horace departed, and Lisbeth went to see how Lara was.

Lisbeth peered into her room. Lara was lying on her bed.

'Hello, Lara, are you feeling sleepy, little darling?'

'No, I feel sad.'

'I understand. Why don't we take a walk in the garden? That might cheer you up.'

'All right, can I take teddy?'

'Yes, of course you can.'

Lara, teddy, and Nanny went downstairs and into the garden. The roses were in full bloom as were the camellias; the perfume was magnificent.

'Can we walk down to the lake, Nanny? I'd love to see the swans.'

'Yes, I think we can do that. Why don't we get some bread from the kitchen, and then you can feed them.'

'Yes, that would be wonderful.'

Lisbeth went back while Lara sat on the grass. It wasn't too long before her nanny returned with the bread.

'Right, we're organised. Let's go.'

They walked down to the far edge of the garden where there was a one-acre lake with a wooden bridge and a small jetty. There was a rowboat tethered to the jetty.

'Darling, why don't we row out to the middle of the lake and feed the swans from there?'

'Oh, Nanny that would be great.'

Lisbeth untied the rope and once Lara was safely seated she pushed off using one of the oars. It didn't take long before beautiful white swans surrounded them.

'They must be hungry! Look how they are fighting to get the bread, Nanny.'

'It doesn't matter how full their tummies are, they'll still fight for every piece of bread.'

Once the bread was all gone, Lisbeth rowed back to the jetty helping the little girl to alight from the dinghy. She secured the boat, and they returned to the manor.

Lisbeth ate her dinner with Lara – the cook had prepared her favourite, shepherd's pie. This would become the standard routine, Lisbeth and Lara eating the evening meal in the dining room. The mansion had two dining rooms: the smaller family dining room where Lisbeth and Lara ate and the grand dining room that held sixty diners.

After dinner, the nanny read from Lara's new book, *The Little Princess* by Francis Hodgson Burnett. The young Countess seemed to be able to relate to Sara the main character. It seemed they had a lot in common.

Lara settled into the new routine well. She seemed to have a happy demeanour although she would often cry when she was alone in her bedroom. Lara missed her mummy and daddy terribly.

The next stage in Lara's life was about to begin: school.

SCHOOL DAYS

CHAPTER 5

St Leonards School for Girls

September 1948

The day arrived when Lara was due to begin her first year at St Leonards Girls School in Somerset only five miles from Westmoreland Manor.

Lisbeth laid her school uniform out on the bed and helped the schoolgirl dress for her big day.

'Are you looking forward to your first day at school sweetheart?'

'Yes, although I'm a little bit scared.'

'Why darling it will be the beginning of a great adventure, you will meet new friends and learn all sorts of things.'

'Yes, but I'm still a little scared.'

'You'll be okay once you settle in.'

Lisbeth called for the driver, John Spencer to bring the car around to the front of Westmoreland so that she and Lara could be driven to St Leonards to begin her new life.

The Rolls pulled into the school entrance, the imposing front gates and gothic building intimidated the young girl she felt like she was going to a prison.

'What's the matter Lara you look afraid. St Leonards is excellent school I know you will enjoy it here.'

'I hope so. I wish Mummy was here with me.'

'She is darling, she's watching over you all the time so is Daddy.'

The car parked close to the main entrance. Lisbeth instructed Mr Spencer to wait while she escorted Lara into the school and introduced her to the headmistress, Mrs Humphries.

The headmistress was a tall woman with red hair worn in a bun. She looked rather stern in her grey woollen suit and practical low-heeled shoes. She had been married to a fighter pilot, Wing Commander William Humphries who was killed during The Battle of Britain in October 1940.

Elizabeth Humphries never married again and she regarded her students as her children.

They waited outside until her secretary announced their presence to Mrs Humphries. The Headmistress came out of her office greeting Lisbeth and the new student and invited them in.

'Well, Lara I'm very pleased to meet you. I know you will enjoy your time at St Leonards. It won't be all learning. There are many sports you can play such as hockey, netball and swimming. I'm sure you will make lots of friends as well.'

'Thank you. Can Nanny stay with me while I'm here?'

'I'm sorry dear, but that wouldn't be possible. Nanny has many things to do before she picks you up at 3 pm. I will take you to your classroom where you can meet your teacher, Miss Cooper, and meet the other children in your class. Say goodbye to Nanny – she'll be back before you know it.'

The Headmistress thanked Lisbeth for taking Lara's hand as she led her through the school's corridors until she reached the First Grade classroom.

Miss Cooper instructed the children to stand as Mrs Humphries entered along with Lara.

'Children this is Lara. I'd like you all to say hello and make her feel welcome.'

The First Grade students all said 'hello' in unison. Lara was shown her desk, a timber top with a tubular steel frame. Although nervous she was beginning to feel more comfortable. The day encompassed drawing, singing and playing with blocks.

At 3 pm Nanny returned to find Lara waiting at the front of the main building along with another girl called Megan. The two girls had already formed a friendship

'Here's my nanny Megan. I better go, see you tomorrow.'

'Goodbye Lara.'

'Hello, darling. How was your first day?' asked Lisbeth.

'It was splendid Nanny. I met a new friend called Megan.'

'That's wonderful.'

Lisbeth and Lara chatted on the short trip home. The nanny was delighted at how her demeanour had completely changed since the morning.

London September 15, 1948

London Middle Temple Lane

The inaugural Trust meeting was due to be convened at Sir Horace's chambers in the heart of the London's legal area, 'The Temple.'

The meeting was due to begin at 3 pm. Mrs Humphries took the train from Castle Cary, the closest station to the school; a two-hour journey.

Mr Harmsworth's offices were in London. A thin man with horn rim glasses, he spoke with a slight stutter but was regarded as a financial genius.

Lord Andrew de Neville, who didn't work at all and never really had in his forty-five years resided in Bath, drove himself in his Aston Martin DB2.

Lord de Neville was born into wealth and used his family's vast resources to purchase expensive cars and travel abroad first-class. His other passion was women, expensive women; Lord de Neville spent large amounts of his wealth on diamonds and expensive jewellery to keep his lady friends happy.

Once all the trust members arrived they were ushered into the chamber's meeting room and seated at the meeting table.

It was magnificent; the panelled walls and portraits of past members of chambers adorned the room. The long table and chairs would have suited a royal household.

Chamber's Meeting Room

Sir Horace called the meeting to order and addressed the trust members.

'As you are all aware, this trust has been established to manage the affairs of Lara de Neville, also known as the Countess de Neville. I think we all agree that our main priority is to ensure Lara receives a proper upbringing and is educated to the highest level.

'Miss Lisbeth Forsyth, Lara's nanny for the past six years, has agreed to continue caring for the girl in the role of legal guardian. I have made application to the court to have her appointment approved. I think we should all be pleased that the young girl will have some continuity in her life.

'I call on Mr Harmsworth to brief us on the financial status of the de Neville estate.'

'Thankyou Sir Horace, ladies and gentlemen. I'm sure you are all aware the de Neville land holdings are quite vast including Westmoreland Manor in Somerset and Raby Castle, in Scotland. A townhouse in South Kensington and a villa in Nice, France are also owned by the estate.

'Currently, the London townhouse and the French Villa are being leased on a long-term basis. As well as the real estate assets the family has an extensive share portfolio together with debentures and Government bonds.

'Finally, the furniture and artworks in the manor and castle are valued at well over a million pounds.'

'Mr Harmsworth, have you been able to estimate the total value of the estate?' asked Lord de Neville.

'At this stage, it is estimated the value of the de Neville estate is around £25,000,000.'

'My God, I had no idea Harry was so wealthy,' said Lord de Neville.

'Well, the family have been building their wealth over the centuries and have been careful managing it.'

'Thank you Mr Harmsworth, the trust has a duty not only to maintain the wealth of the estate but to grow it until Lara is entitled to her inheritance at age 18,' said Sir Horace.

'Sir Horace, will the members of the Trust get remunerated for the time spent on Trust business?' asked Mrs Humphries.

'Yes, all members will be paid at the same rate, £50 pounds an hour. I arrived at this figure based on my standard hourly rate for estate management. I would expect Mr Harmsworth and I will spend the most amount of time on trust business; you and Lord de Neville will be remunerated for the meetings attended, including travel time.'

'Are there any implications for the estate regarding death duties?' asked Lord de Neville.

'No, the law stipulates that if a minor is under 18 and a trust has been established, there's no inheritance tax if the assets in the trust are set aside just for bereaved minor, i.e. Lara.

'It is also dependent on Lara becoming fully entitled to the assets by the age of 18.'

'She shall be a very wealthy young lady.'

'Indeed, she will be Lord de Neville.'

'I understand that Lara will continue to reside at Westmoreland but what should we do with the other properties?' asked Mrs Humphries.

'Raby Castle is situated on 200 acres of prime farming land, it is more than self-sufficient, and therefore I think the property should be retained. The London townhouse and the Nice villa are both being leased and generate excellent revenue. Therefore, I recommend the property portfolio be retained.'

'Thank you Sir Horace, I agree,' said Mrs Humphries.

'As you all are aware Mrs Humphries is headmistress at St Leonards Girl's School in Somerset. We are not only fortunate to have her as a trustee she will also be reporting on Lara's progress, both scholarly and mentally at each meeting.

'Miss Forsyth has made a request to the trust. Apparently, Lara's father promised her a pony upon his return from America. Miss Forsyth requires a sum of £200 to purchase a suitable pony plus tack. Are we all in agreement?'

All trust members nodded their approval.

'Good. Mr Harmsworth, would you be kind enough to transfer funds to the house account, please.

'Well, I think we have finished business for this meeting. May I suggest we meet again in December unless there is urgent business that requires attention.'

THE COUNTESS AND PRINCESS

CHAPTER 6

Lisbeth was notified that the trust had approved the purchase of a pony for Lara to ride the grounds of Westmoreland. There were extensive horse trails winding through the estate, more than enough to keep a girl and her pony happy.

Lisbeth made her way to Westmoreland's large oak barn where she knew Mr Bryant would be at this time of day cleaning the stables and providing fresh hay for the twenty thoroughbred horses owned by the de Neville estate.

'Mr Bryant may I please have a word?'

'Certainly, Ma'am.'

'Firstly I think we should address each other by our Christian names at least while we are alone.'

'Sounds fair to me, Lisbeth.'

'Excellent, Peter. Now what I want to talk to you about is finding and acquiring a pony for young Lara.'

'I see, do you have any particular breed in mind?'

'I believe a Connemara pony would be an excellent choice.'

'You've chosen well Lisbeth. The Connemara is an intelligent, manageable, and exceptionally kind pony. Perfect for a young beginner.'

'The trust has allocated £200 for the pony and tack. Do you think that will be enough?'

'That should just about cover it. So do you want me to go ahead and find a suitable animal?'

'Yes please, I'm sure you'll choose the right horse.'

A week had passed by when Lisbeth received a telephone call from Peter Bryant informing her of the purchase of a Connemara pony with a full tack for £180. Lisbeth was delighted. She wanted to keep it as a surprise for Lara but knew it would be difficult to keep the news to herself for too long.

The pony arrived at Westmoreland stables on Friday, September 7 and Peter housed it in a stall next to the most placid horse in the stables, Bonnie.

The next day the nanny suggested to Lara that they take a walk to the stables and say hello to the horses. This was a regular occurrence and one that Lara enjoyed immensely.

'Nanny, take a look in this stall it seems there is a new pony.'

'Oh isn't it beautiful. I wonder if it's a girl or a boy?'

'Judging by its pretty face I'd guess it's a girl.'

'Can I pat it, Nanny?'

'Why don't I ask Mr Bryant to take it out of the stall then we can both pat it.'

'Yes, that would be great.'

The caretaker put a bridle on the pony and led her out of the stall so Lara could get close. Both Peter and Lisbeth were touched by the affection Lara showed the pony.

'What's her name, Mr Bryant?'

'Well, that depends on what you decide to call her.'

'What does he mean, Nanny?'

'He means that this is your pony darling. You choose a name.'

'Mine, are you saying this is my pony?'

'Yes that's right, it's yours.'

'Mummy and Daddy promised me a pony when they came home from America. They must be home!'

Lara left her pony and ran out of the stables heading for the manor. She was sure her parents had returned from America – they weren't in heaven after all. Lisbeth followed her into the house. The excited girl was running from room to room calling out for her mummy and daddy. Finally, she slumped on the floor crying.

'Lara darling it's all right Mummy and Daddy are still in heaven. They wanted you to have the pony so whenever you take her for a ride, you will think of them.'

'I always think of them Nanny – I miss them.'

'I know you do, we all do.'

Lisbeth stayed with Lara consoling her until she asked to see the pony again. They walked to the stables and up to the stall where the pony was once again housed.

'I'm going to call her Princess, that's what Daddy called me.'

'That's a lovely name she looks like a princess.

Lara and her nanny went riding through the estate at every possible opportunity, the young girl on Princess and Nanny on Bonnie.

Lara enjoyed her first year at St Leonards Girls School. She made many friends. However, her best friend remained Megan, who she met on her first day at school.

She was coping well with her lessons and she also excelled at sport. However, the orphan girl was still grieving for her parents.

December 1948

The students in Lara's class put on a Christmas play for parents and family in mid-December. She played one of the three wise men and looked the part with colourful flowing robes and a full beard. Although she enjoyed being part of the pantomime, the young orphan was conscious that her Mummy and Daddy weren't in the audience applauding. Her nanny attended, but it wasn't quite the same.

St Leonards broke up for the Christmas holidays on December 20th and snow was falling when Lisbeth arrived in the estate's car. Mr Spencer the Westmoreland driver opened the door for the young countess, and they made their way back to the estate.

'So darling, are you looking forward to the holidays?' asked Lisbeth.

'I think so although I'll miss seeing Megan and the other girls.'

'Well, I have a surprise for you! Megan will be coming to visit us on Boxing Day and staying for a whole week.'

'Really that would be wonderful, thank you, Nanny. We'll be able to go riding together. The only thing is she won't have her pony.'

'Yes, she will. Her Daddy will be bringing her pony when he drops Megan off.'

'That's great1 I can hardly wait.'

December 25, 1948

A typical Christmas for Lara would encompass waking up constantly throughout the night, sneaking downstairs to check under the tree to see whether Santa had been. Finally, about 6 am she would discover many brightly wrapped presents; it was then that she would run back up the stairs knock on her parent's bedroom door announcing excitedly that 'Santa has been!'

This Christmas was different; Lara slept through the night and in the morning it was Lisbeth who knocked on her bedroom door to announce Santa had been.

Although she received some wonderful presents including a new saddle, she wasn't that excited. Lisbeth sadly looked on knowing that this little girl would take some considerable time to get back to normal, whatever normal was.

Christmas lunch was served on the long table in the dining room and all the staff and their families attended making the occasion a joyous one.

December 26, 1948

Lara was more excited about Megan arriving than she had been about celebrating Christmas. She kept checking the driveway looking out for a car with a horse float. Finally, at 2 pm, Megan arrived. Both her father and Lisbeth were amused to see the two girls hugging each other and talking to each other at the same time. Lisbeth was sure not a single word was heard or understood by either of them.

Lisbeth suggested that the girls and Megan's father, James Whitlock, should come into the house for afternoon tea. Lara and Megan couldn't sit still and Lara asked Nanny if they could go outside to help put Megan's pony in the stables. Peter Bryant had unloaded the pony called Star and was taking her to join Princess.

'Hello, Mr Bryant, can we help you with Star?'

'Yes, certainly Lara and who's your little friend?'

'This is my best friend Megan. She's come to stay for a week. Star is her pony.'

'Well, we better introduce Star to Princess.'

'Yes, I hope they become good friends,' said the excited girl.

The two girls and Peter led Star into the stables and placed her in the stall next to Princess.

'Now young ladies, I think it best that we leave them like this until the morning. It'll give them a little time to get acquainted. Tomorrow we'll get them out, and you can go for a ride together.'

'OK I can hardly wait,' said Lara.

'Either can I,' agreed Megan.

The two friends returned to the house and Lara showed Megan where she would be sleeping. Lisbeth had arranged for an extra single bed to be moved into the bedroom.

After dinner, they shared a bath and dressed in their pyjamas ready for bed. Lisbeth came up to their room and read *Rebecca of Sunnybrook Farm*. Both girls were asleep by the time Lisbeth finished the second chapter. Lisbeth looked down on the two sleeping beauties. She was so pleased Lara had met such a good friend after all she had been through.

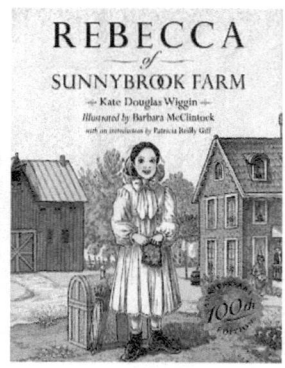

The next morning after breakfast the two friends asked Lisbeth whether they could go riding. She agreed on the condition that she and Bonny accompany them.

The three horse lovers dressed in their riding outfits including helmets and made their way to the stables. Peter Bryant was mucking out the stalls.

'Good morning, Mr Bryant. We'd like to take the ponies out for a ride. Would you be good enough to help the girl's saddle up?'

'Certainly, ma'am.'

Bryant led Princess out first. When she was saddled he tied her to a post and then fetched Star. She was a little jittery and difficult to saddle up. Megan went over and stroked the pony's neck and nose. Star responded, calming down.

Once the three horses were saddled Mr Bryant assisted the two girls to mount their ponies, and Lisbeth led them out on Bonnie. She decided to take the trail which ran down by the river – it was a relatively easy ride.

Apparently, Princess resented Star being on her turf and she attempted to bite the other horse anytime Megan tried to ride side by side with Lara. Lisbeth suggested they ride single file to alleviate the problem. They were riding through a wooded section when Megan moved too close to Lara and Princess. The pony kicked Star in the chest with both hooves causing Megan's mount to rear up. Megan lost her balance, falling off the pony. She was wearing her riding helmet but she hit her neck on a tree stump. Lisbeth dismounted immediately as did Lara: Megan was unconscious. Lisbeth checked her neck for a pulse. There was one albeit very faint.

'Lara, you stay here with Megan just stroke her hair and keep talking to her. I'm going to ride back to the house and get help.'

'Don't be long.'

'I'll be as quick as I can.'

Lisbeth mounted Bonnie, riding as fast as she dared along the track. She arrived at Westmoreland hoping she would find Peter. He was working in the front garden.

'Peter! Quick! Get the Land Rover. Megan's had a fall and needs to get to the hospital as soon as possible.'

'My God.'

They ran to the machinery shed and leapt into the Land Rover driving as fast as he could over the uneven terrain. Eventually they reached the two girls. Lara had her friend's head in her lap, stroking her head and crying, pleading for Megan to wake up.

'Lara we need to get Megan to the hospital quickly let me take her. You sit in the backseat,' Lisbeth instructed.

'I'll tether the horses and return later to bring them back to the stable,' said Peter.

Peter drove back to Westmoreland and then onto the recently opened Musgrove Park Hospital five miles away. On arrival, Lisbeth carried the still unconscious girl into the emergency ward. A doctor took her immediately, however, it was too late – Megan had died on the journey to the hospital. She was classified as 'Dead On Arrival.'

The doctor who made the pronouncement listed her cause of death as a vertebral artery dissection that led to a subarachnoid haemorrhage.

Lisbeth sat next to Lara in the emergency waiting room put her arm around the little girl and whispered in her ear that her best friend had gone to heaven.

Lara's reaction was unexpected she got up and yelled.

'It isn't fair!'

She ran from the emergency room. Fortunately, Peter was having a cigarette outside on the footpath. He called out to her. She stopped and lay down on the nature strip, crying. Lisbeth appeared and again lay down beside her grieving charge trying to console the little girl. Lisbeth couldn't care less that they were outside a busy hospital – Lara was her main concern.

Lisbeth and Peter managed to convince the grieving girl that they should go home. They drove the five miles listening to Lara sob – it was gut wrenching.

When they arrived, Lisbeth took Lara into the kitchen to make her chamomile tea. This scenario was becoming all too familiar; surely this was enough grief for a little girl to bear.

Peter returned to the scene of the accident with a horse-float loading the two ponies together; this could be a problem, he thought, but they were behaved. They possibly sensed that their animosity to each other had caused the accident.

Upon arrival at the manor, he noticed a police car parked outside the portico. He decided to take the ponies back to the stables; the police would seek him out if they needed to talk to him.

Lisbeth encouraged Lara to go to her room while the police interviewed her about the accident.

The police took Lisbeth's statement and asked where the accident occurred. Lisbeth explained she couldn't leave Lara alone but suggested Peter guide them to the scene.

The caretaker drove the two police officers in the Land Rover to the spot where Megan was thrown from her horse. After examining the area, they were satisfied with Lisbeth's statement as to how the accident occurred.

The next task for the police was to notify Megan's parents. This was a task most police dreaded.

Sad Lara

Chapter 7

The days following Megan's death were tough for both Lara and Lisbeth; the young girl became withdrawn, spending much of her time in her room. Her nanny tried to encourage the forlorn girl to spend time outside in the garden, but she was met with indifference. Lara had not been near the stables to see Princess since the day of the accident. The days turned into weeks, and the weeks turned into months without much change in her emotional state. She was now back at St Leonards Girls School and was under the watchful eye of Mrs Humphries. The headmistress reported to the trust on the young heiress's progress at the March trust meeting in London.

'Welcome everybody, as you know Lara has experienced another terrible blow and is having difficulty coping. I would like to table Lisbeth Forsyth's report for your consideration. I now call on Mrs Humphries to present her report,' said Sir Horace.

'Thank you Sir Horace. Yes, Lara is going through a very tough time at the moment. She not only lost her parents but now she has lost her best friend. I have been keeping a close watch on her at St Leonards and have noticed how withdrawn Lara has become. She is pleasant to her classmates but won't let any of them get close to her. Lara has lost all interest in sport and only partakes in the compulsory games during physical education classes.

'One consolation is she has dedicated herself to her schoolwork and therefore is achieving excellent results.'

'Do you have any recommendations that would help her get back to normal, as it were?' asked Lord de Neville.

'My opinion is she needs to interact with girls of her age.'

'Isn't that was she's doing at your school?'

'Yes, but she needs more. My recommendation is she enrols at our boarding school – she will be in constant company with similar-aged girls, plus have the benefit of guidance from the older boarders and teachers.'

'What do we all think of Mrs Humphries' recommendation?'

'My view is we need to consult with Miss Forsyth first before any decisions can be taken,' said Mr Harmsworth.

'Yes, I'm sure you're right Arnold,' said Sir Horace.

The trust members agreed that Sir Horace would visit Lisbeth Forsyth and discussed the options with her.

The following week Sir Horace contacted Lisbeth and arranged a meeting at Westmoreland.

1949

Cuba recognises Israel

Joe Di Maggio becomes the first $100,000 a year player

The Peoples Republic of China proclaimed by Mao Zedong

March 31, 1949

Sir Horace's car drove up the tree-lined driveway to Westmoreland and parked under the large portico. Sir Horace eased himself out of the back seat stepping onto the paved pathway. He looked around at the magnificent gardens: 'This would be difficult to leave,' he thought.

Lisbeth met him at the front door inviting the portly solicitor inside. They made their way to the library.

'Can I offer you a cup of tea, Sir Horace?'

'That would be lovely, Miss Forsyth.'

Lisbeth rang the kitchen placing her order that included scones jam and cream.

'So, where's young Lara?'

'She's in her room where she spends a large part of her time these days.'

'So it's been difficult for her, no doubt?'

'Yes, as you would expect.'

'The trust has asked me to get your opinion on whether you think it would be beneficial to her recovery to become a weekly boarder at St Leonards.'

'I take it 'weekly' means she would come home on weekends?'

'That's correct. The trust members believe it is important that she remains connected with you and her home. Mrs Humphries has made the recommendation on the basis Lara would be living with girls her age and could, therefore, come out of her shell.'

'When would she be expected to begin boarding?'

'At the beginning of next term.'

'Would you mind very much if I gave it some thought before giving you my opinion?'

'Not at all, Miss Forsyth. Take your time.'

Sir Horace finished his tea and devoured the last remaining scone before taking his leave.

Lisbeth thought long and hard about what would be best for Lara. Eventually, she came to the same conclusion that the trust had made; it would be in her best interest to attend boarding school.

She telephoned Sir Horace, agreeing to the trust's proposal.

'I must ask you Sir Horace: with Lara attending boarding school will my overall salary package remain the same?'

'Certainly Miss Forsyth, have no fear. It's just as important to the girl and the board that you remain at Westmoreland. She will be home every weekend and of course term holidays.'

'Thank you. I was a little concerned I would no longer be required.'

Lisbeth's responsibility was to inform Lara of the change to her living arrangements. This she knew would be difficult for her to accept.

At dinner, she broached the subject.

'Lara, I have something important to talk to you about.'

'What is it, Nanny?'

'Well, Mrs Humphries your headmistress and the other trust members that look after your interests have decided that the best thing for you would be to become a boarder during the week and come home on the weekends.'

'Why? I like living here with you and Lucy, Mr Bryant and the others.'

'Darling, you will be living with your classmates. You'll have so much fun together. On the weekends we can do all the things you like doing, like rowing the boat along the river and horse riding together.'

'I don't think I ever want to go horse riding again.'

'You may change your mind in the future, you never know.'

'When will I have to start?'

'The beginning of next term in a few weeks.'

'If I don't like it can I come back home?'

'Yes darling, of course you can.'

'All right. I'll give it a try.'

BOARDING SCHOOL

If you don't eat your meat you can't have any pudding.

CHAPTER 8

July 1 1949

Lisbeth organised Lara's suitcase with the clothes she would need during her first week at boarding school. Also, packed were her favourite toys and her favourite picture book *Petunia*. Lara loved this silly goose.

Lisbeth collected the suitcase and went downstairs to meet Mr Spencer, who placed the case in the boot and waited beside the car.

Lara was in the kitchen enjoying a glass of orange juice and a freshly baked scone with jam and cream. Her nanny waited patiently for the girl to finish her treat. Finally, she was ready to take the journey to St Leonards.

The St Leonards girl was familiar with the routine, but this time she wouldn't be making the return journey until Friday afternoon.

Once they arrived at the imposing school, Lisbeth accompanied Lara to the Headmistress's office where Mrs Humphries greeted them.

They walked to the boarding school dormitory, Mrs Humphries leading the way. The headmistress showed the nervous new girl her bed and explained the cabinet next to it was where she was to store her possessions.

Lara's Dormitory

The room was stark compared to her room at Westmoreland. There were four iron beds, each with a chest of drawers but nothing much more adorned the room. In her room at home she slept in a beautiful cream four-poster bed, and not only had a chest of drawers but also had an ornate dressing table with three mirrors. She also had a large doll's house with lots of dolls and toys.

'I don't think I'll like it much here,' she thought.

It was time for Lara to join her class and reacquaint herself with her classmates after the long break.

Lara was not what you would call the most popular girl in the class; she tended to keep her own company and not make friends easily. She created a wall around herself, determined not to be hurt again.

The young student enjoyed her classes which allowed her to concentrate on things other than her sad life. At the end of the school day, when most of the other girls were either picked up or rode home, Lara and the other boarders returned to the boarding school for afternoon tea. After tea, they had sports activities for ninety minutes. Lara once again enjoyed playing hockey and tennis.

The evening meal was served in the dining room at 6 pm, and then the girls went to the library where they were required to complete their homework. This was the regime that Lara and the other boarders followed each weekday except for Fridays. Lara always looked forward to seeing Mr Spencer waiting to take her back to Westmoreland for the weekend. This feeling of euphoria was offset by the sense of dread when Mr Spencer returned her to St Leonards on Sunday afternoon.

Life as a boarder continued uneventfully. She had been eagerly awaiting the Christmas break, when Lisbeth and her cousin Andrew were going to take her to Raby Castle, in Dundas Scotland. The de Neville family had owned the magnificent castle for centuries.

Mr Spencer was waiting for the eager young girl standing beside the car. As usual, it was he who would be driving the family to Scotland. He was as excited as Lara: he loved spending time at the castle and more importantly, hunting for deer in the estate's magnificent woodlands.

The car pulled up under Westmoreland's portico where Lisbeth was waiting to greet Lara.

'Good afternoon, young lady, are you pleased to be on holidays?'

'Yes, of course, Nanny who doesn't like being away from school? I'm looking forward to Christmas too.'

'Well, come inside. Lucy baked your favourite today – scones.'

'Yummy.'

Lara sat down at the long kitchen table while Lucy the cook placed scones on a plate together with some made strawberry jam freshly made from strawberries grown in the manor's vegetable garden and freshly whipped cream from the small dairy located on site.

'Lara, as you know we'll be travelling up to Raby Castle this holiday.'

'Yes, Nanny. I'm so looking forward to it.'

'How would you like it if we went early and spent Christmas day there?'

'That would be great.'

'Right, well that's settled. We leave tomorrow.'

Lisbeth spent the remainder of the day organising Lara's suitcase and the extra provisions they required to celebrate Christmas at Raby Castle.

She telephoned Andrew de Neville to inform him they would be leaving for Scotland the following morning. He had no problem with the new arrangements and promised to meet them at Westmoreland at 8 am the next day.

December 24, 1949

Andrew arrived on time. Mr Spencer loaded the car and the group left for Scotland at 8.30 am. Mr Spencer estimated the journey would take 8 hours including a lunch stop.

The limousine parked in front of the magnificent 14th-century castle just on 5 pm, it had been snowing for the past few days and the grounds looked beautiful.

'Nanny it looks wonderful! This will be my first white Christmas.'

'It's been a long time since I enjoyed a white Christmas, Lara,' said Andrew.

'How long is it since you were last here, Andrew?' asked Lisbeth.

'Gee, it must be ten years, I used to come here once or twice a year.'

'Did you come here when my Daddy was here?'

'I certainly did, your Dad and I were the best of friends. We explored the whole castle more than once.'

'Maybe you could take me exploring.'

'Yes, I'm sure I can.'

'Well, come on everybody let's get inside. It's cold out here!' said Lisbeth.

The drawing room had a fire lit and a servant brought in hot chocolate for the newly arrived guests.

Drawing Room Raby Castle

'Nanny, how will Santa know we are here?'

'Don't worry darling. I wrote him a letter.'

'Oh good, I'm hoping he will bring me a bike.'

'You never know.'

Lisbeth, Andrew, and Lara ate dinner in the small dining room which also had a fire; in fact there were more than thirty fireplaces in the castle.

The nanny put Lara to bed and read her a new book *The Enchanted Castle* by E Nesbit – a very appropriate title she thought.

Lara woke early, keen to discover if Santa had found her at the castle, and crept downstairs looking in all the rooms she could find. The rooms were enormous – Santa could have left the presents anywhere. Lisbeth heard the little girl and followed her downstairs.

'Has he been yet?'

'I don't think so, Nanny. I can't find any presents. Not even under the Christmas tree.'

'Did you look under the tree in the library?'

'No, I didn't think to look there.'

'Well, come on. Let's have a look shall we?'

The two of them crept into the library just in case Santa was still there. Lara let out a little scream.

'Look Nanny! He's been! Look at the presents! And Nanny he's brought me a bike!'

The red bike was a three-wheeler driven by a chain, exactly what she had hoped for.

Lara sat down on the floor and started to open her Christmas presents: there were books, dolls, and lots of new clothes. She was so excited.

Once all the presents were looked at fondled and admired it was time for Christmas breakfast. Andrew joined them bearing gifts for both Lara and Lisbeth.

Over breakfast they decided they should build a snowman at the front of the castle. It needed to be a fast build as the temperature outside was -15 degrees Fahrenheit.

Once the snowman was completed Lara asked Andrew if they could go exploring; he agreed.

Initially he took her through the castle's main rooms.

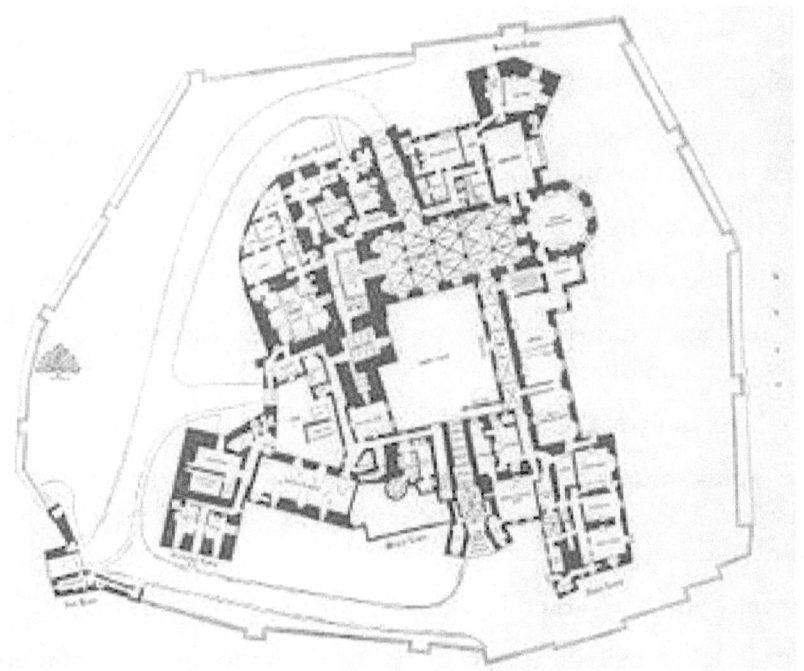

Floor Plan Raby Castle

They made their way through the ballroom and the various sitting rooms, the large kitchen and the banquet room. Finally, Andrew asked Lara whether she would like to see the dungeon. She didn't know what a dungeon was but agreed. Carrying a torch, Andrew took her hand and led her down a dark stairway.

Stairway Leading to the Dungeon

Lara pleaded with Andrew not to move any further down the dark, cold stairwell.

'I don't like it here. Can we please go back?'

'There's nothing to be frightened about darling. I'm here. We're almost at the end. Then we can explore the dungeon.'

'I don't care. I want to go back.'

'All right, maybe we can explore it another time.'

Andrew and Lara returned to the sitting room where Lisbeth and Mr Spencer were enjoying a cup of tea.

'Well, you two, did you discover anything interesting?' asked Lisbeth.

'Yes, we pretty much covered the entire castle. Lara saw pictures of her ancestors, and I showed her the bedroom where her father and I slept when we were here as boys,' said Andrew.'

'Did you enjoy it, Lara?' asked Lisbeth.

'Yes, but I didn't like the staircase going down to the dungeon much, I became frightened.'

'Andrew you didn't take her down there did you? No wonder she became frightened.'

'Harry and I went down there all the time when we were young boys.'

'Young boys and seven-year-old girls are entirely different. I ask you not to take Lara down there again.'

That was the last they spoke of it. Lisbeth had a surprise for Lara after lunch she hoped she would respond well to it.

No hour of life is wasted that is spent in the saddle.

Winston Churchill

Chapter 9

Lisbeth and Lara walked around to the stables behind the castle the estate kept twenty racing thoroughbreds. The nanny had arranged with Westmoreland's caretaker Peter Bryant to bring Princess up to Raby a couple of days before Lara and she arrived. She hoped that Lara would begin riding the pony again. She hadn't seen Princess since the day of Megan's fatal accident.

'Darling, would you like to see the horses – they're beautiful?'

'I don't mind. I suppose so.'

They walked into the magnificent stables where Peter was feeding the horses their oats.

'Hello ladies, have you come to help me?'

'What do you think, Lara? Should we help Mr Bryant with the feeding?'

'What do we need to do, Nanny?'

'Well, we just fill the feed troughs with oats.'

'So we don't have to go in with the horses?'

'No darling, we just fill the box from the outside of the stall.'

'All right. I'll try.'

'OK, pet, just take some oats from the bag and place them inside the feeding box,' explained Mr Bryant.

'There. I did it, he seems to like them. Look how he's gobbling them up,' said Lara.

'Would you like to feed another one?'

'Yes.'

'Why don't we feed the horse at the very end of the stable. I'm sure she's hungry.'

'All right then.'

The three of them walked to the end of the stable where a pony was restless in the stall, waiting to be fed. The little girl stopped in her tracks looking at the pony – she didn't approach it.

'That's Princess. I'm not feeding her.'

'Why not darling?' asked Lisbeth. 'She's your pony – you loved her.'

'She killed Megan.'

'Lara, it was a terrible accident. Princess didn't mean to hurt her.'

'If it weren't for her Megan would still be alive.'

'OK, sweetheart let's wander back to the castle and have afternoon tea. As they both left the stable Lisbeth looked back over her shoulder at Peter. He shook his head.

After dinner, Lara asked to be excused. She went to her bedroom and lay on her bed. She tried to come to grips with Princess being in the stable and whether it was the pony's fault that Megan was killed. She thought of all the wonderful times she and her pony had had, riding through the grounds of Westmoreland. Lara remembered how she used to groom Princess and feed her apples. They were the best of friends.

Lara finally concluded that Princess was only a pony and didn't know any better. She would ask her nanny if they could go riding the next day, but not on the river trail.

In the morning at the breakfast table, Lara announced her decision.

'Nanny I've decided I would like to take Princess for a ride today if that's OK.'

'Why yes darling that would be wonderful. What changed your mind?'

'I don't think Princess meant to kill Megan. It was an accident.'

'I know. You're right, sweetheart. Princess is a lovely pony. It was just one of those things. I'll contact Mr Bryant and have him saddle up our horses.'

Lisbeth and Lara made their way to the stables. Mr Bryant had saddled up Bonny and Princess and both horses were champing at the bit. Neither had been ridden for some time.

Once they had mounted their steeds they walked towards the Heather Moorlands where they could experience a comfortable ride. The young horsewoman had no desire to trot or canter; she preferred to walk Princess until she became more confident on the pony. The ride took an hour and back at the stables, Lara expressed her delight and indicated to her nanny a desire to ride again the following day.

Horse riding became a daily routine during the holiday at Raby Castle. Each day brought increased confidence to Lara, who by the end of the week was cantering around the estate on Princess who also enjoyed the exercise.

The Christmas holiday came to a close. They all returned to Westmoreland and Lara returned to boarding school.

Born in the USA

Chapter 10

1950

India becomes an independent republic

Walt Disney's *Cinderella* released

First kidney transplant (USA)

January 1950

Lara returned to boarding school at St Leonards in the second week of January 1950. She wasn't looking forward to sharing a dormitory with three other girls after sleeping in her bedroom at Raby Castle. Mr Spencer and Nanny dropped the young student off at the front of the building and Lara carried her suitcase into the austere room and placed it on her bed. There was a girl sitting on the bed beside Lara's. Lara had no idea who she was but as far as she was concerned that bed belonged to Kathryn.

'Excuse me but you're sitting on Kathryn's bed,' said Lara.

'I was told by Mrs Humphries that this was my bed.'

'Oh I see, are you new?'

'Yes, my name is Jane.

'I'm Lara.'

'I've just arrived from America.'

'Oh.'

'Did you come here with your mummy and daddy?'

'Yes, of course, I did. They are living in London. I'll go home every weekend.'

'That's like me. I go home every weekend.'

'Where do you live?'

'Not that far from here.'

'What do your mummy and daddy do?'

'They're dead. They died in America.'

'Oh no, I am sorry.'

'That's all right. You weren't to know.'

The two young boarders became friends. Iit was the first time since Megan had passed away that Lara had allowed herself to form a close friendship.

Not only did they talk at night after lights out, but they would play in the school grounds at lunchtime every day. Jane was also learning to play tennis and she and her new friend would practise together on the school tennis courts.

Lara and Jane became inseparable, sharing all their innermost secrets.

As the years passed they remained the closest of friends and Jane became a regular visitor, not only to Westmoreland but also Raby Castle.

The American girl became a keen horsewoman riding along the trails with her best friend at both de Neville properties.

Lara would also visit Jane and her parents at Richmond Park in London where they would visit the museums and art galleries and it was during these visits that Lara discovered her love of art.

1959

Alaska admitted as 49th US state

Buddy Holly killed in a light plane crash

The USA recognises Fidel Castro's Cuban government

Both Lara and Jane graduated from St Leonards with A-Levels. Neither of them achieved dux, but they weren't far off it. The next stage in their young lives would be University – Jane was accepted at Oxford studying law while Lara was accepted to study medicine, also at Oxford.

Both young ladies chose accommodation in Jesus College where they had their own bedrooms while sharing a living room with separate study areas. For a building, that was built in the 17th century it was very comfortable.

1960

Elvis Presley admitted into US Army.

Jimmie Hendrix had his first gig.

Triton submarine completes first submerged circumnavigation of the earth.

The girls didn't just share rooms at Oxford, they shared a love of music; Lara had the latest stereo record player.

Their favourites ranged from Elvis Presley singing *It's Now or Never* and *Are you Lonesome Tonight*, to Chubby Checker singing *The Twist*, and The Drifters *Save the Last Dance For Me*.

The following year it was Ben E King *Stand by Me*, Del Shannon *Runaway*, and The Marcels *Blue Moon*.

Their world changed in 1963 when both of them turned twenty-one, and a new group released their first single: *She Loves You*. From the first time they heard the Beatles they became their biggest fans. They saved their allowances with the sole purpose to buy every Beatles record.

1963

The French conduct underground nuclear test in Algiers

Alcatraz Closes

Winston Churchill appointed the first ever honorary US citizen

Jane graduated with honours and hoped to join a law practice in San Francisco: Orrick was a firm that was established in 1863. Her mother had returned to the USA the previous year after her husband had died from prostate cancer in Britain.

Lara was devastated; her closest friend would no longer be there for her. She had another year of study before she completed her medical degree. She had been considering taking a year off when she completed her degree, intending to visit Jane in San Francisco.

The two young women decided they would go to a Beatles concert as the last farewell. The Fab Four were playing at the Wimbledon Palais in London on December 14.

When Lara and Jane arrived at the venue, they couldn't believe the number of fans milling outside the theatre. The Palais had a maximum capacity of 3,000 but Jane was sure there had to be 5,000 people outside the venue.

'OK girlfriend, they've opened the gates. Get your ticket ready and be prepared to run for the stage,' said Jane.

'This is going to be like a buffalo stampede. I hope we make it without being trampled,' said Lara.

The two Beatles fans ran for the stage the concert organisers had erected a steel cage to protect the band from their fans.

The young women were fortunate enough not to be at the front pressing against the cage – if they had been they could have been injured. The crowd was mostly teenage girls screaming and pushing forward despite the band being absent from the stage.

The announcer came on.

'Ladies and Gentlemen the Wimbledon Palais is proud to present to you THE BEATLES.'

Pandemonium broke out. If the crowd were out of control prior to the band stepping onto the stage, it was hysterical now. Before the Beatles sang a note, young girls were fainting. The Palais staff was having trouble keeping up with the number of young girls that required medical attention.

Finally, the crowd heard the four idols shout.

'HELLO. WE'RE THE BEATLES.'

The first few bars of *Money* got the crowd even more hysterical and so the concert went on, with the Beatles playing their entire latest album *With the Beatles*.

Being older, Lara and Jane were frustrated at not being able to hear the group clearly over the screaming but still enjoyed being there and seeing their idols.

December 18

Lara drove her friend to Heathrow Airport to catch the plane back home. She helped with the luggage and then stood in front of her best friend in the baggage drop area.

'I'm going to miss you, darling. You make sure you come over after your final year and stay with me,' said Jane with a tear in her eye.

'I will, I promise.'

'Goodbye, dear friend.'

'Goodbye, Jane. I love you, sweetheart.'

The two friends hugged each other for what seemed like an eternity and then bade their final farewell.

1964

Lyndon Johnson declares war on poverty

Cassias Clay converts to Islam and renamed Muhammad Ali

Australian Destroyer Voyager sinks after colliding with aircraft carrier HMAS Melbourne killing 82 sailors

Oxford 1964

Lara made the decision to move out of the university accommodation she shared with Jane. She found a one-bedroom flat close to the campus, which was expensive, but very comfortable. Money was not a problem for this student – she was one of the richest women in Britain.

Lara committed herself to her final year: no more parties or concerts, just study. Although she sorely missed her friend Jane, the final year medical student utilised the time effectively, which resulted in her excelling in her studies.

December 1964

Lara had completed her final year and was looking forward to the graduation ceremony. The Head of Medicine, Professor James Ford had informed the young graduate she had been awarded the Margaret Harris Memorial Prize, a much sought-after honour for excellence.

Lara at Graduation

Now, Lara had another title to add to her name: Doctor. Several London hospitals offered her an internship, however, the young doctor decided she would keep to her original plan and go to San Francisco to stay with Jane in her beautiful 'Painted Lady.'

OPPORTUNITY KNOCKS

CHAPTER 11

December 1 1960

Lord Andrew received a telephone call from his good friend and old school chum from Eton, Lord Geoffrey Arthur.

Despite the two men attending different universities – Lord Arthur attended Cambridge while Lord de Neville attended Oxford – they remained close friends.

'Hello Andrew, it's Geoffrey. Have you got a minute to chat, old boy?'

'Always got a minute for you, old chum. What's up?'

'I've been lucky enough to come across an investment that I think you may be interested in.'

'I'm always on the lookout for a sure thing Geoffrey. When can we discuss it?'

'Well, I thought we could meet at our club tomorrow lunch time. We could have a bite to eat, and I can fill you in.'

'Yes, that sounds good. What time?'

'Say 12 noon.'

'I'll see you there.'

The two aristocrats were members of 'Whites', a gentleman's club located in St James Street, London. Established in 1693, it is one of the oldest and most exclusive clubs in England.

White's Club

Lord de Neville arrived at noon to find Lord Arthur already waiting in the smoking lounge.

'Take a seat Andrew. Would you like to join me in a cigar? I believe they're Cuban.'

'Thank you Geoffrey. Very kind of you.'

'So how's that beautiful wife of yours?'

'I'm afraid we're no longer together. We split up in July.'

'Oh, I am sorry to hear that chum. You seemed so happy together whenever I saw you both.'

'I thought so too, but apparently she didn't. She ran off with some Australian and now she's living in Sydney.'

'Well, at least you don't have children to worry about.'

'That's true, although as you know, I've taken on some responsibility for my young cousin who became an orphan when both her parents died in a boating accident in America.'

'Yes, I was aware of that. How old is she now?'

'She was six when she was orphaned. She turns 18 next birthday.'

'So she lives with you?'

Andrew explained the role of the trust and how Lisbeth Forsyth became her legal guardian.

'She's quite the young lady now, beautiful and soon to be very wealthy. She still lives at Westmoreland Manor in Somerset with Lisbeth Forsyth. They have a very strong bond.'

'You mentioned her impending wealth?'

'Yes, when she turns 21 in September 1963 she becomes the sole heir to the de Neville fortune.'

'Have you any idea how much the estate is worth?'

'I do, but I'm not at liberty to discuss it. Let's just say she will be one of the richest women in Great Britain.'

'Well, if you've finished your cigar shall we go into the dining room?'

'Yes, why not?'

The two men entered the lavish dining room and were seated by an elderly waiter.

'Would you care to see the menu, sir?

Both men scanned the menu deciding on the same main course, eye fillet with a pepper cream sauce.

'So Geoffrey what is this investment you wish to discuss with me?'

'You would remember my father no doubt? He was a very wealthy businessman.'

'Yes, I only met him the once, but I know of his reputation.'

'As you know he died two years ago but it's only now that I've become aware of his true wealth. It's taken this long to unravel the structure of his business empire.'

'So you've inherited a fortune?'

'No, not exactly. It seems towards the later part of his life he made some very strange and how shall I say it – 'dodgy' business decisions.'

'So where does that now leave you?'

'One of the good decisions he made was to buy a resources based company. The company has North Sea oil leases as well as 50 per cent of a diamond-mining venture in Angola and a gold mining lease in Western Australia.'

'My God it must be worth a fortune.'

'Not presently, but it will be. That's where you and other possible investors come in. The potential is enormous, but it needs investment to allow all three to come into full production.'

'How much money are you hoping to raise?'

'I'm putting up £10,000,000. I need to raise a further £10,000,000.'

'What sort of return do you expect?'

'I honestly believe investors will receive 30 per cent in the first year.'

'My God, that's enormous! Are you sure?'

'As sure as I've ever been in my life.'

'Geoffrey, what's the name of the company?'

'No offence Andrew but I can't tell you until you have committed to the venture. If word got out it could prove disastrous.'

'How much would you like me to commit?

'That's up to you old chum. Whatever you feel comfortable with.'

'Do you mind if I give it some thought?'

'Not all, but don't take too long. As soon as I reach the target I'm closing down the prospectus.'

'I'll get back to you by the end of the week. I just need to work out my finances.'

'Excellent, now do you feel like having a dessert?'

'No thank you I've had enough to eat.'

The two friends bade farewell, with Andrew recommitting to get back to Geoffrey by the end of the week.

Andrew returned to his Kensington townhouse to determine how he could raise the money to invest in Geoffrey's company. He sat in his office and wrote down some figures.

Kensington Town House

de Neville House, Padstow, Cornwall

Kensington Town House	£3,000,000
Padstow house	£1,500,000
Shares	£1,000,000
Cash reserves	£100,000
Total	£5,600,000

Andrew knew it would take some time to dispose of the properties; besides, he wasn't keen to do so. He decided to use them as collateral for a loan. The next decision was where to borrow the money. He was regarded as part of the British establishment and wasn't keen to approach his bank, Barclays, or any of the other major banks, as he preferred to keep off the credit radar.

Andrew had had some dealings with a merchant bank in Australia, Nugan Hand. They charged a higher interest rate but lent money more freely than the British banks. He decided to contact them the following day.

After submitting his asset statement, Nugan Hand agreed to lend him £4,000,000 using the two properties plus his share portfolio as security.

Andrew felt that this was worth the risk, as the investment would return £1,200,000 after only one year. His intention was to hold onto the investment for five years.

He decided he would go ahead and telephoned Geoffrey with his decision.

'Hello, Geoffrey, it's Andrew. I've made up my mind. I'm in.'

'Well done, old boy! How much would you like to invest?'

'Put me down for £4,000,000.'

'Jeepers, are you sure you want to invest that much?'

'I know you can't guarantee the return, but your word is good enough for me.'

'Well, Andrew the next move needs to be we get together to sign the papers and celebrate with a fine malt whisky and a cigar.'

'That sounds like an excellent idea. When would you like to meet?'

'It will take the solicitors a few days to prepare the paperwork – how about we make it at your place next Monday?'

'That suits me. What time?'

'What about 4 pm?'

'Done.'

'OK, we'll see you next week. Goodbye, Andrew.'

'Goodbye, Geoffrey.'

Geoffrey arrived at the Kensington townhouse on time. Andrew's butler answered the door and showed Geoffrey into the study. Andrew joined him soon after.

'Good afternoon Geoffrey. Can I offer you a drink?'

'Hello, Andrew. Why don't we get the business out of the way then we can enjoy the malt I brought to celebrate our partnership.'

'Yes, that sounds like a splendid idea.'

'I have brought you the papers to sign. You may wish to have your solicitor run his eye over them first?'

'Unnecessary, old fellow. I trust you implicitly.'

'As you wish. You will see that your investment entitles you to 200,000 shares in Riqueza Investments, which equates to 20 per cent of the company.'

'Ah, at last. I learn the name of the company that will make me even wealthier. It sounds Spanish.'

'It is. *Riqueza* is Spanish for 'wealth', one of my father's quirky names.'

'Well, I hope that is an omen.'

'I'm sure it will be.

'Andrew, when will you be able to deposit the funds?'

'Tomorrow if you like. Give me your bank account details, and I'll transfer the money.'

'Excellent!'

'I think it's time to open that bottle of whisky and smoke a cigar.'

'Sounds good to me. What whisky did you bring?'

'The *Macallan* 25-year-old and to go with it a *Montecristo* #2.'

'Both are my favourites.'

The two friends sat in the fine leather wingbacks drinking their malts and smoking their Cuban cigars. The talk centred on the plans to develop Riqueza's enormous resources.

After they had each consumed three glasses of malt, it was time for Geoffrey to call a taxi and return to his Park Lane home. Andrew returned to his study and drank another whisky before taking a nap before dinner.

The next day he reviewed his investment. He had no remorse. He had borrowed the money from Nugan Hand at the rate of 10 per cent and expected a rate of 30 per cent from Riqueza giving him a net return of 20 per cent. He knew he would have to dispose of some shares to pay the interest in the first twelve months but after that, it would be plain sailing.

Life was starting to turn around for the young Lord.

Dirty Rotten Scoundrel

Chapter 12

Lord Geoffrey Arthur returned to his apartment feeling very pleased with himself. He had secured another four million to add to his current total of £30,000,000 that he had raised from friends and business colleagues.

He had no upper limit in mind; he would continue to raise capital for his fictional mining company until the Ponzi scheme came to its natural conclusion…collapse. By that time he would have transferred millions of pounds away in Switzerland and the Cayman Islands. His final plan included faking his disappearance and living on an island in the Pacific – he was leaning towards the Cook Islands.

Because Riqueza Investments was supposedly a private company, he could create positive progress reports which he would distribute to investors every three months.

RIQUEZA

Diamonds

The pipes that had been dug in Lucapa Angola are showing signs of high-grade diamonds with an estimate of 50,000 carats at deeper drill levels.

Oil

Oil exploration in the North Sea is looking extremely promising. The Block allocated to Riqueza is regarded as one of the richest Blocks so far allocated by the British Government.

Gold

Our geologists have discovered gold seams in the Eldorado mine that potentially could produce 300,000 ounces a year.

The reports became more and more positive, potential investors referred by existing investors were knocking on Geoffrey's door begging for him to allow them to invest. Who was he to deny them?

The early investors, including Lord Andrew de Neville, were beginning to receive their dividends. They weren't disappointed, the return on investment averaged over 30 per cent. They weren't to know that Arthur was paying them from the investment money of others, not from oil or diamonds or gold. It was a massive Ponzi scheme that would rock the British establishment.

1 December 1964

Lord Arthur knew it was time to wind up the scheme. After all it had been going for four years. He had raised £50,000,000 and paid out £20,000,000 in dividends, but some investors were beginning to question the credibility of the company. He had gotten wind that a journalist from *The Times* was planning to visit Angola and Australia to investigate how viable the mines were and if in fact, they existed at all.

He transferred the remainder of his funds held by British banks to Switzerland and the Cayman Islands and a reasonable amount to the Cook Islands. He then drove his Aston Martin to Beachy Head in East Sussex, one of the most notorious suicide sites in England.

He removed his shoes – why he did nobody could understand – and jumped off the infamous cliff. That's what he wanted everybody to believe.

A local alerted the police, and a search was done at the bottom of the treacherous cliff, but the body was never found.

Geoffrey had plastic surgery in Thailand and then immigrated to the Cook Islands where he lived in relative luxury until his death in 1987.

Andrew first learnt about the massive swindle when he read about it in *The Times*. He was sitting in his office planning a trip to Australia. He had never been down under and thought it would be an ideal holiday, visiting the Great Barrier Reef and Sydney Brisbane and Melbourne, as well as the gold mine in Kalgoorlie in Western Australia and then flying home via Asia.

He was devastated. The debt owing to the bank was £4,000,000 and he knew there wasn't a hope in hell of repaying it. The properties in London and Cornwall would be sold from under him; his cash reserves had been used to pay the quarterly interest payments on the loan so effectively he was broke.

The dejected gentleman poured himself a large whisky and contemplated his future. The glass was empty and he still had no idea what he could do to try to resurrect his life. He poured another. A glimmer of an idea began to evolve.

If Lara died, he would be the last remaining heir to the de Neville fortune. No, he couldn't bring himself to arrange a hit on his beloved cousin; after all, he had been one of her guardians since she was six. From that initial thought, he developed a new plan. He could arrange for Lara to be kidnapped; a ransom of £5,000,000 would be demanded. Lara would remain safe and would be released once the ransom had been paid. No-one would get hurt, and he knew the trust had the resources to pay. Lara would still be left with her extensive property portfolio and a share portfolio more than £3,000,000 after the ransom had been paid.

Andrew knew he had hit on the right solution. All he had to do now was plan the exercise meticulously, right down to the finest detail.

He wrote a list.

1 Find two villains to kidnap subject

2 Determine best location to imprison subject

3 Determine where the ransom can be left and then retrieved safely

4 Feed and water subject without being identified

5 Work out how ransom notes won't be traced

6 Money will be bulky investigate other means

'That will do for now,' he thought.

Lord de Neville retired for the night but he had trouble sleeping and kept thinking about the kidnap plan. He was quite excited about the whole adventure.

In the middle of the night, he sat up in bed and said to himself: 'That's it! The secret chamber at Raby Castle.'

He knew the dungeons and catacombs of the castle better than anybody. He and his cousin Harry, Lara's father, had spent many summers exploring the chambers and tunnels that ran under the castle.

'I can put Lara in one of the secret chambers. Perfect! We don't need to take her outside the castle where she may be seen.'

Over the next month Andrew developed his plan and was now at the point where he was ready to implement it.

He reviewed his original plan:

1 Find two villains to kidnap subject

Mr X & Mr Y are confirmed. A payment of £10,000 each has been agreed.

2 Determine best location to imprison subject

Secret chamber at Raby Castle

3 Determine where ransom can be left and then retrieved safely

The ransom will be lowered down well in the town square in 'Dundoon' Use secret escape tunnel to access the dry well.

4 feed and water subject without being identified

Use mask and not communicate with Lara.

5 Work out how ransom notes cannot be traced

The ransom will be paid in uncut diamonds to the value of £5,000,000

Andrew was satisfied with all the aspects of the kidnap. He would start by suggesting to Lara they visit Raby Castle. The object of the visit would be to teach Lara how to shoot grouse. She had often mentioned to him how she would like to learn how to hunt.

KIDNAPPED

CHAPTER 13

1965

Who's first album *I Can't Explain* released

South Vietnam military coup under General Nguyen Khanh

Sir Winston Churchill dies

Tuesday, 1 March

Lara was having wine with Lisbeth in the back courtyard. The two women were very close; after all Lisbeth had been Lara's legal guardian since she was six and now that she was 23 they were like mother and daughter. Lara let very few people get close to her; the two closest were Lisbeth and Jane, her American friend from boarding school.

The women were discussing plans to travel to Raby Castle with Andrew who'd offered to teach Lara how to hunt for grouse. Although Lisbeth was going, she had no intention of shooting the magnificent birds – she'd rather paint them, which had become her passion. Her paintings of English and Scottish wildlife had become quite popular in art galleries in Britain and abroad.

'I received a phone call from Andrew this morning. He's decided to drive himself up to Raby instead of going with us. Apparently, he may have to return to London for a day; something to do with urgent business,' said Lara.

'OK. That's fine. Are we taking your car?'

'I'm dying to have a decent run in the Mini Cooper.'

'Well you know what a nervous passenger I am, no driving like Fangio.'

'Don't worry Lisbeth, I'll take it easy.'

The two women left Westmoreland at 9 am the following morning. It would take them the best part of the day to reach Raby Castle.

They stopped for lunch at a quaint little pub called the Bobbin Mill in Buckshaw Village. Both women enjoyed a Ploughman's Lunch and were on their way again 45 minutes later.

It was late afternoon when the red Mini Cooper arrived at the castle. Lara parked next to Andrew's silver Aston Martin.

Andrew came out to greet them and help with the luggage. Once the two ladies were settled into their rooms they joined Andrew for wine in the observatory overlooking the magnificent gardens.

'Andrew, what plans do you have for me tomorrow?'

'If she only knew' he thought. Well the first thing you need to learn is how to handle a shotgun. I've set up a clay pigeon launcher in the far garden so you can learn how to shoot and reload. Once you've got that mastered, we can drive out to the heather moorlands at the far end of the estate the following day. I've organised four dogs to retrieve in the hope they'll have birds to fetch.'

'Of course, they'll have birds to retrieve Andrew! I'll be an expert shooter by then.'

'Yes, I'm sure you will be, Lara.'

'What about you Lisbeth? Are you going to join us?'

'Not likely. I'll stay here and do some sketching.'

'May I suggest we find out what chef has in store for tonight's dinner,' said Lara.

'Excellent idea.'

What chef had in store was roast venison shot the day before by the castle's gamekeeper, Mr Campbell. It was delicious. Andrew chose a 1959 *Montlouis Cabernet Franc* to accompany the meal.

Lara and Lisbeth were both feeling the effects of the long drive, and the wine, so they both decided to retire early. This suited Andrew's plan. He figured they should both be asleep by 10 pm when the two degeneratess were due to arrive at the castle via a secret tunnel, one of ten the castle boasted. The two sleeping pills he slipped into Lisbeth's wine would also help his cause.

The one part of the plan Andrew was not looking forward to was being bashed. He knew it must appear that he had been assaulted when the police arrived. He descended to the catacombs to ensure everything was prepared for Lara's imprisonment. He had set up a camp stretcher with two blankets and a pillow. There was also a large container of drinking water. Although it contained enough for three days, he intended to replenish it daily along with fresh food. He also installed a camp toilet and a washbowl and two hurricane lamps: he didn't want Lara to be in constant darkness.

The kidnapper was Satisfied that he had thought of everything, the kidnapper ascended to the library where he had arranged to meet Mr X and Mr Y. He had no need to know their names and felt it best not to. He had two parcels of 100-pound notes amounting to £20,000. It was a lot of money, especially now that his wealth had been reduced to virtually zero, but he knew it would be worth it.

He entered the library to find the two men sitting in the leather wingbacks smoking and enjoying one of the fine malt whiskies from the drinks cabinet.

'Well, I see you've made yourselves comfortable.'

'Hello Gov. Yeah, it's nice 'ere. No wonder you want to get rid of the girl.'

'I don't want to get rid of her. Now get up! I hope you remember what you need to do. Let's run over it again.'

'Right Gov. Well, we sneak up to the girl's bedroom and hold a pistol to her lovely 'ead. We gag 'er and tie 'er hands and take 'er down to the dungeon. We lock 'er in and make sure the stone flap covers the keyhole. We then give the key back to you.'

'No, no! You take the key and throw it away when you leave. Preferably in a river. I have a duplicate.'

'Right then.'

'What next?'

'We come back up quietly so we don't wake the other one. We enter your bedroom and we pistol whip you but not too hard. We tie you up like a turkey and gag you.'

'That sounds right. Unfortunately.'

'When do we get our dosh?'

'When you come up to my room and confirm you have locked her away.'

'Fair enough. Well you better go up to your bedroom and wait for us to pay you a visit.'

'Yes, I'm looking forward to it.'

Lara was sleeping soundly. She was woken by the two scoundrels wearing black balaclavas. One put a hand over her mouth to stop her screaming while the other tied her hands.

'Right, me lovely! We won't 'hurt you unless you scream. If you do, we're going to 'ave to strangle you. That wouldn't be very nice, would it?

Lara shook her head.

'Now then, I'm going to take my hand away from your mouth. Remember – scream, and I kill you.'

Mr X took out a cotton scarf and stuffed it into Lara's mouth and another scarf was wrapped around her head acting as a blindfold.

'Ok girlie, ease yourself out of bed. We're all going for a little walk.'

The men escorted Lara down into the catacombs and placed her in the secret chamber, a place she was familiar with from her exploring with Jane. They took out the gag and untied her hands. Finally they removed the blindfold.

'Why are you doing this? I've done you no harm?'

'Sorry darlin', we can't tell you. I don't think you'll be in here long so just relax and enjoy.'

The door was shut with a clang, and Lara was left to contemplate her fate.

'What in the hell is going on? Why have they kidnapped me?' The feeling of claustrophobia began; the stone walls were closing in on the young heiress.

It was cold in her prison cell, yet beads of sweat ran down her beautiful face. It was fear, not the heat that made her perspire.

Lara paced up and down the small space she would call home for who knows how long. Rats scurried along the flagstones, spiders climbed the walls. Not a very pleasant environment.

'Whoever is behind this knows about my wealth. I haven't told any of my friends except for Jane. It wouldn't be her – she loves me. It could be one of the Trust members? No, they've always looked after my interests.'

Lara lay on her camp stretcher and sobbed. She feared for her life.

The two men crept up to Andrew's bedroom and entered without knocking.

'Hello Gov, she's all locked up nice and tight.'

'You didn't hurt her, did you?'

'No Gov, we treated with kid gloves.'

'Good, now what do you want me to do?'

'Why don't you lie on the bed and shut your eyes. I'll just stick this hankie in your mouth – we don't want to wake up the lady next door do we?'

Andrew nervously waited for the first blow. Mr Y pistol-whipped him across the face. He decided that wasn't quite enough so he whipped him a second time. Andrew was bleeding profusely over the pillow and sheets.

'Right then. You look a right mess, Gov! That should convince the cops. Now we'll tie you up good and proper but before we do that we want our money.'

'It's in the wardrobe over there.'

'Well done. Well, put your 'ands above your 'ead and we'll truss you up.'

Once Andrew was suitably restrained the two villains grabbed their money and left the castle by the same tunnel.

Wednesday 2 March, 1965

Lisbeth was seated at the breakfast table in the conservatory eating her muesli and wondering where the others were. They had agreed to meet at 9 am before Lara's first shooting lesson. At 10 am she decided to see whether she could rustle them up. She knocked on Lara's bedroom door, but there was no reply. Entering; she discovered Lara was not in her room.

The strange thing was that Lara's outfit, the one she intended to wear shooting, was still neatly laid out on her dresser.

Lisbeth then knocked on Andrew's door and heard no reply she knocked again calling out his name. A faint mumbling sound was heard. Lisbeth decided to enter his room. What she discovered shocked and horrified her.

Quickly she removed the gag. All Andrew uttered was 'untie me'.

Once untied, he tried to explain to the bemused woman what had happened. Lisbeth immediately returned to Lara's room for closer inspection and found an envelope under her pillow. There was a letter inside.

Lara has been kidnapped.

If you wish to see her again you must follow our instructions.

The ransom is five million pounds, to be paid in uncut diamonds.

There will be a notice in the personals of The Scotsman newspaper on Saturday 5th where you will learn where the drop will take place on Sunday at 7am.

The add will be placed by Millie Basset.

Call the police, we don't care

The Socialist

Lisbeth sat down on Lara's bed she couldn't believe this was happening. Poor Lara, what she was going through?

She looked up to see Andrew at the door bloodied and dishevelled.

'What's wrong, Lisbeth? Where's Lara?'

Lisbeth handed Andrew the ransom note. He read it then slumped down on the bed next to Lisbeth.

'My God! I can't believe it. So that's why those thugs beat me and trussed me up like a turkey. So I couldn't intervene.'

'We need to call the police immediately.'

'Yes, we do. I'll call them.'

'No, you're in no condition to handle this. I'll call them.'

Lisbeth quickly went downstairs to call the police. Once she had reported the kidnapping and answered the officer on duty's questions he assured her a patrol car was on its way.

Andrew didn't clean himself up. He felt it was important that the police saw how badly he had been beaten by the evil kidnappers. He made his way gingerly down the stairs and entered the library where Lisbeth was waiting for the police to arrive.

'Lisbeth, did you hear anything last night? After all I was beaten, and Lara was taken.'

'I'm sorry Andrew. I promise you I didn't hear a thing. I wish I had.'

They both heard the doorbell; Lisbeth went to allow the officers in. Three police officers entered the library, two uniformed and one detective.

'Good evening. My name is Chief Inspector Russell, and these two constables are Jones and Cook. May I ask you to take a seat? What I would like from both of you is a verbal statement of what you saw and experienced last evening. We'll take a written statement from you both later on.'

'With due respect, Chief Inspector, shouldn't you be trying to find Lara? She still could be close by?'

'Madam, I've had twenty years in the force I think I know what I'm doing. The kidnappers will be well and truly gone by now, and the victim will be imprisoned in a very secure place.'

'Sorry Chief Inspector. It's just horrible that some beast has taken my Lara. I feel there must be something we can do to find her.'

'Fear not madam, we will do everything in our power to find Lara. The first thing I would like to see is the ransom letter.'

Lisbeth took the letter from her trousers pocket and handed it to the inspector. He read it carefully then gave it to PC Jones to be added to the newly created file.

'Have either of you heard of The Socialist?'

'No, sounds like a communist plot. You don't think it's the Russians, do you Chief Inspector?'

'Hardly.'

Both Lisbeth and Andrew recounted what they knew about the sequence of events leading to the kidnapping.

'They certainly gave you a beating, Lord de Neville. Why do you think they targeted you and not Lisbeth?'

'I have no idea Chief Inspector. I suppose they thought being a man I might hinder their plans. You know, put up a bit of a fight.'

'And would have you?'

'I love my cousin Chief Inspector. I would do anything to protect her.'

'OK. PC Jones will take down your written statements and then we'll be on our way.'

'So what happens now?'

'I'm afraid we are going to have to wait until Saturday's newspaper and see what this Millie Bassett instructs us to do re the ransom. We will make enquiries around the traps to see if any of our informants in the criminal world have any idea what's going on.'

'Thank you Chief Inspector, we do appreciate your support,' said Andrew.

'Yes, thank you,' said Lisbeth.

Lisbeth showed the police officers out and returned to the library where Andrew had poured himself a whisky.

'It's a bit early for that isn't it?'

'I don't care. With all that's happened I need a drink.'

'I can't believe these kidnappers are making us wait until Saturday before we know what they want us to do.'

'I know, it's very frustrating. Why don't you head back to Westmoreland and look after things from that end and I'll stay here.'

'I will if you don't mind.'

Lisbeth drove Lara's Mini back, taking a full day to complete the journey. The trip home was vastly different from the trip up to Scotland with Lara.

With Lisbeth out of the way, Andrew thought it would be much easier to look after Lara.

He wore a balaclava to disguise his identity and didn't speak to his cousin; he used written notes to communicate with her.

Apart from the anxiety, she felt she was in reasonable spirits and good health. Andrew fed her with fresh fruit, cheese and bread. He refilled her water bottle each day.

One request Lara had after 24 hours in captivity was for some books to read; she was sick of looking at stonewalls.

Anthony was a keen reader so grabbed three recent books he had read:

The Spy Who Came In From the Cold –John Le Carre

Planet of the Apes – Pierre Boulle

On Her Majesty's Secret Service – Ian Fleming

They weren't the type of books Lara read, but she was grateful for the distraction.

DIAMONDS ARE FOREVER

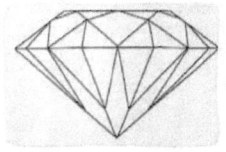

CHAPTER 14

Saturday March 5th

THE SCOTSMAN

Personal

To Whom It May Concern:

The parcel is to be placed in the bucket of the village well at Dundoon and lowered down.

Sunday at 7am

Millie Bassett

Chief Inspector Russell and his team read the notice with interest. He dispatched PC Jones to the village of Dundoon to inspect the well and determine the vantage points where he and his colleagues could view the drop-off point.

Village Well

Chief Inspector Russell contacted Sir Horace to discover whether the trust had been able to raise the ransom. Sir Horace confirmed that they had disposed of £5,000,000 in blue chip shares and De Beers agreed to convert the cash into uncut diamonds. As far as the trust was concerned, it was ready for the ransom to be paid.

The only decision to be made was who would make the drop. The kidnappers had not specified a particular person.

Chief Inspector Russell drove to Raby Castle where he would stay until after the ransom was paid and hopefully an arrest was made.

He arranged to meet with Andrew to go over the details of the plan.

'Well Lord de Neville hopefully we will bring back Lara to you and arrest the villains tomorrow.'

'I pray that you will Chief Inspector.'

'Would you be prepared to make the drop?'

'Oh, I don't think so. I'd be afraid I'd stuff things up. I would never forgive myself if I did.'

'No bother, I'll do it.'

Andrew breathed a sigh of relief. He had other things he needed to do that morning.

The two men ate a light meal together and retired for the night. It would be a big day for both of them.

Andrew went over the plan in his mind. He needed to enter the tunnel at 6.30 am and knew from his rehearsals that it would take twenty minutes crawling through the tunnel to reach the bottom of the well. He would wait until he heard the bucket being lowered. Once he had retrieved the diamonds, he would hide them in a secret compartment in a chest of drawers in his bedroom.

He knew it was essential that he remained in the castle continuing the charade of being the distraught relative awaiting news from the police.

The following morning he would call the offices of Sir Horace from a telephone box ten kilometres away in the village of Gairloch, informing him where Lara was imprisoned and where he could find the key, which he had hidden behind a book in the library. He thought his choice of book was ironic, *Kidnapped* by Robert Louis Stevenson.

All good, Lara would be free with no real harm done, and he would retain the wealth he had been accustomed to all his adult life. He would welcome Lara back with loving arms. No-one would be any the wiser, including the police.

Sunday, 6 March

Andrew had a very fitful sleep; he tossed and turned all night, eventually rising at 5 am. He arranged a clean set of clothes, which he would change into once he returned from collecting the diamonds. They were duplicates of the outfit he would wear to breakfast that morning. Once showered and shaved he joined the Chief Inspector for breakfast.

'Good morning Lord de Neville. Did you sleep well?'

'No, not really. I was thinking about all the things that could go wrong.'

'Don't worry. I'm sure we have everything covered.'

'Did the diamonds arrive last night?'

'Yes, they're locked away securely until we make the drop.'

'Excellent.'

The two men ate their breakfast in silence. At 6.15 am the Chief Inspector excused himself to check on his officers' surveillance positions.

Andrew wished him luck. Once the Inspector had departed he made his way down below the castle and into the chamber where the well tunnel was located.

Tunnel Leading to Well

He crawled to the end of the tunnel and waited anxiously. The luminescent hands on his Rolex showed it was 6.55 am.

At 7 am he heard the bucket being lowered halfway down. He could see it slowly making its way until it reached the bottom of the well.

Andrew lifted the ten-kilo bag from the bucket and tentatively peered inside. It wasn't just a bag of dull translucent stones – this was his salvation.

He quickly returned to Raby Castle and hid the bag in the chest of drawers before returning to the library to play the anxious cousin.

Chief Inspector Russell had placed ten police officers in various surveillance positions surrounding the town square where the well was located. He was concerned: what self-respecting kidnapper would place themselves in a position where to collect the ransom would require them to not only be in the open but to pull a heavy bucket up to the top of a deep well? It just didn't make sense.

7 am came and went without any movement once the diamonds had been lowered. Another fifteen minutes passed and still no action. After half an hour Senior Inspector Russell called off the operation.

'Nothing's happening, bring the bucket up,' he instructed PC Jones.

The constable began winding up the bucket. He knew at once it was empty.

'Sir, it's empty. There's virtually no weight in it.'

The bucket arrived at the top. Empty. Pandemonium broke loose. Russell and his men were totally dumbfounded.

'Maybe the bucket tipped over when it hit the bottom of the well. Jones, I need you to go down there and find out what the hell is happening.'

'Yes, Sir.'

Two other police officers helped Jones straddle the bucket; they slowly lowered him down. He had his police torch to provide some light.

When he reached the bottom of the well, he could not see the bag but what he did discover was the entrance to the tunnel. Using his walkie-talkie, he related his discovery to his superior.

'Jones, follow the tunnel to see where it leads.'

'Yes, Sir.'

The young police officer began his journey, ever conscious of the countless rats scurrying around and the sound of bats flying past.

When he reached the end of the tunnel, he entered a large chamber with spiral stairs leading up to goodness knows where.

'Sir, can you hear me?'

'Yes. But you're very faint. What have you discovered?'

PC Jones described what he had found.

'Stay where you are Jones. I'm sending another man down to support you.'

Chief Inspector Russell directed PC Cook, Jones's partner to go down the well and join his comrade at the end of the secret tunnel. Cook completed the journey and found his partner sitting against a stone wall in the cold dark chamber.

'I don't like it much here mate. Bit too eerie for my liking,' said Jones.

'I know what you mean. Let's climb those stairs. Maybe we can get out in the open.'

The two police officers began climbing the stone stairs, about thirty in all. They came across a thick wooden door. Thank God it was unlocked.

The two constables looked at each other with trepidation. Jones gingerly pushed it open. They couldn't believe their eyes as they stepped out into a beautiful courtyard. On inspection, they discovered they were in the grounds of Raby Castle. PC Jones tried to contact Chief Inspector Russell, but the walkie-talkie was out of range.

It took the two young men thirty minutes to walk down to the village.

'Sir, the tunnel leads to a courtyard garden in Raby Castle.'

'Did you find anything suspicious?'

'No, Sir.'

'Right then. Everybody back to the station except for Jones and Cook. You come back with me to the castle.'

The three police officers drove the patrol car to Raby Castle, parked near the front door and rang the doorbell. A staff member answered the door showing them into the library where Andrew was waiting.

'Good morning, Lord de Neville.'

'Good morning Chief Inspector. Did you catch the bastards?'

'No, I'm afraid they got away with the ransom.'

'What the ... ! How in the hell could they get away? You had the square staked out.'

'They used a secret tunnel to access the well.'

'Do you know where it leads to?' asked Andrew.

'Here.'

'What? Raby Castle?'

'Lord de Neville, are you aware of this tunnel?'

'No, I know there are secret tunnels, but I've never heard of a tunnel leading to the well in the village.'

'Can you think of anybody that would have knowledge of such a tunnel?'

'Chief Inspector the castle has employed many people over the years. It would be impossible to determine who had access to this information. I'm sorry, but I'm more interested if the kidnappers left a note describing how we can free Lara.'

'I'm afraid not we haven't received instructions from the kidnappers as yet.'

'So what happens now?'

'We wait to hear from the kidnappers. In the meantime, who on the castle staff has access to the employee records?'

'I'm not sure. I think Lisbeth would know.'

'I haven't seen her recently. Where is she?'

'She drove back to Somerset.'

'I wish she had informed me of her plans. I'll try calling her at Westmoreland tonight. There's nothing more that we can do other than look for clues in the tunnel. I'll leave PC Jones here to complete the search.'

'What are you going to do, Chief Inspector?'

'I'm needed back in Scotland Yard. I'll return when we have heard from the kidnappers.'

'Safe trip.'

'Thank you.'

Once the Inspector departed, Andrew made arrangements to drive to Gairloch to telephone Sir Horace to inform him where the key and a map to find the secret chamber were located.

He slid onto the kid leather driver's seat and began his short but arduous journey to the village. The roads were notoriously windy with near vertical drops into the rocky valley below. Andrew was in a euphoric mood – he had the diamonds and Lara would soon be free unharmed. He was also feeling very pleased with himself as he had pulled off the perfect crime. As he neared a particularly sharp bend, his wheels hit the gravel.

The Aston Martin slid over the edge and plummeted down the cliff face hitting a large pine tree that crushed the driver's side of the car. Andrew died instantly.

Lara's Karma

Chapter 15

Lara was lying on the camp stretcher wondering when the mysterious kidnapper would be bringing her more provisions and fresh water. She had no perception of the time or when he had last visited her. What she did know was that she was starving. At least she still had a reasonable supply of water.

Lara had completed reading the three books, which was just as well as the lamps had run out of kerosene. She was in total darkness. An intense darkness she had never experienced before.

She tried to sleep but was too distressed.

The days passed, Lara drew weaker, drifting in and out of consciousness.

Monday, 7 March

A milk van driven by Alan Scott was heading up the mountain road intending to deliver milk and other dairy products to the Dundoon General Store. As he rounded a particularly tight bend he noticed gravel across the road, and tyre marks disappearing over the side. Parking the car as best he could without obstructing the road, he alighted from the van and looked over the edge. What he saw shocked him: a car had apparently gone over the edge and smashed into a large conifer. Alan knew it would be impossible to survive such a horrific accident.

The milkman continued his drive up the mountain and pulled up outside the general store fifteen minutes later.

'Mrs Lamont there's been a horrible accident on the Gairloch-Dundoon Road. Can I use the telephone to call the police, please?'

'How horrible! Yes of course you can, Alan.'

Alan rang the police at Gairloch, giving them a description of what he had discovered. The police arrived within the hour and a search and rescue officer abseiled down the cliff only to find Lord Andrew de Neville dead in the driver's seat. On the passenger's side was a notebook, which the police officer took on the basis that it might help identify the deceased driver, as he found no wallet on the victim.

Upon reaching the road, he showed his sergeant the notebook. The sergeant read the pencilled notes, alarmed:

Call Sir Horace Winterbottom to inform him where the key and map are hidden to release Lara.

Contact Frederich Kriel re disposal of the diamonds.

The officer immediately radioed the station.

The Gairloch Police Station contacted Chief Inspector Russell at once and a constable was dispatched to Raby Castle with the notebook.

Raby Castle 3 pm

Chief Inspector Russell returned from London and rallied his men together in the castle's large dining room. He knew they didn't have much time, nor did Lara.

'We have a significant problem. We now have proof that Lord de Neville was the perpetrator of this hideous crime.'

'Do we have any idea where he might be, sir?'

'We do. He's in the Edinburgh morgue. His motor vehicle was found this morning at a bottom of a ravine. He was on his way to telephone Sir Horace Winterbottom to disclose Lara's whereabouts and how to release her.'

'How do we know that, sir?'

'He had a notepad in the car with a 'To Do List'. The call was on top of that list. We must find Lara soon as we have no idea about her state of health or whether she has food and water.'

'Do you have any ideas, sir?'

'My strong suspicion is she is incarcerated in Raby Castle. The castle has a myriad of secret tunnels. My understanding is there are also secret rooms. This is a 14th-century building – goodness knows what lies below us.'

'Sir, should we contact all the staff who have worked in the castle over recent years? They may be aware of such secret rooms,' suggested Constable Wilson.

'Good thinking, constable but that would take some time. And that's a commodity we don't have.'

'Sir, may I suggest we contact the major newspapers and television stations. I'm sure they would cooperate. That would give us the maximum amount of coverage in the least amount of time,' said Constable Jones.

'I think you're right I'll contact police media and get them on to it immediately.'

Most of the major newspapers ran with the story, including several overseas papers from America, Europe and Australia.

All the television stations throughout Britain reported the kidnapping in their news telecasts.

San Francisco March 8

Jane Lucas, Lara's closest friend, was eating breakfast in her Victorian 'Painted Lady' house, which she had purchased the previous month. She was able to afford the house from her share of her father's estate.

Painted Ladies

Jane was reading the *San Francisco Chronicle* when a story jumped out at her.

Oh my, God, it's Lara; on reading the story she knew what was required. She telephoned the contact number listed in the article. It was 4 pm in Edinburgh.

'Hello, may I talk to Chief Inspector Russell please?'

'May I ask what it's regarding?'

'I'm a very close friend of Lara de Neville's. I may have some valuable information concerning where she may being held captive.'

'Please hold the line.'

Jane didn't have to wait long.

'Hello, this is Chief Inspector Russell. How can I help you?'

'Chief Inspector, my name is Jane Lucas. I'm a very close friend of Lara de Neville. Lara and I would often visit Raby Castle. We played in the castle's catacombs. We discovered a secret chamber during our adventures.'

'Can you come to the station or better still Raby Castle and show us where this secret chamber is located?'

'I'm calling from San Francisco.'

'Oh, well there must be some way we can get the details from you, Jane.'

'Inspector it would almost be impossible to describe its location. I need to fly over and show you.'

'Jane, I don't know how long we've got.'

'Let me check with the airlines and see when I can be in Edinburgh.'

'OK, I'll wait for your call.'

Jane was able to book a flight direct to Edinburgh with British Airways first-class on 9th March. She telephoned Chief Inspector Russell informing him she would be arriving at 4.40 pm on the 10th.

9 March

San Francisco International Airport

Jane departed San Francisco at 4.15 pm; the flight would take 12 hours and she was thankful she had decided to fly first-class.

Despite the comforts she enjoyed on the flight Jane felt exhausted on her arrival at Turnhouse Airport Edinburgh. She passed through immigration and customs without incident. Upon entering the arrivals hall, Jane noticed a man holding a sign with her name written in large letters. She approached him.

'Hello, I'm Jane Lucas. I assume you are Chief Inspector Russell?'

'Good afternoon, Miss Lucas how was your flight?'

'Exhausting.'

'We have a two-hour drive in front of us. You can shut your eyes and have a nap on the way if you like.'

'Hardly, I'm keen to find out what has been happening and how poor Lara has ended up locked in a cave.'

'A cave?'

'Yes, if she's in the secret chamber we discovered as girls it's virtually a cave.'

The police officer recounted the series of events since Lara was kidnapped.

'Did you ever meet Lord de Neville, Jane?'

'I did, several times. He always seemed so protective of Lara. I find it very difficult to believe he was the kidnapper. Why would he do such a thing?'

'Money, Jane.'

They reached Raby Castle in the early evening. Jane led the police down into the catacombs as soon as they arrived.

'I know it's down this tunnel. I'm just not sure exactly where. There's a symbol of a cross etched into the stone. It's difficult to see, but it's here somewhere.'

'All right, everybody listen up. Spread yourselves along the tunnel. We're looking for a small cross which is etched into the stone.'

The twelve police officers, together with Jane and Chief Inspector Russell, began their search along the tunnel using torches to assist them. After an hour they were still searching.

'I think we will need a stronger light. Constable, go back to the station and grab the arc lights.'

'Yes, sir.'

At that moment, a yell from the far end of the tunnel echoed through.

'I've found it! I've found the cross,' a young police officer yelled.

The search team congregated in front of the wall where the cross had been found. It was very faint, probably due to the fact it had been etched into the stone over 300 years before.

Jane went up to the wall and measured five hand widths down from the cross. She moved her hand across the wall, eventually finding the keyhole cover. She slid the cover to the left, and sure enough there was a large lock.

'Lara can you hear me? It's Jane,' she screamed.

'I don't think she can hear you Jane. These walls are far too thick,' said Chief Inspector Russell.

'So let's break the door down and get her out,' pleaded Jane.

'It's not going to be that easy. First we have to break through the stone and then through the wooden door. I'm going to call in search and rescue. They have all the gear we need.'

'Well, just do it!'

Search and Rescue were on standby and they arrived twenty minutes later. Using a pneumatic hammer they broke through the stone uncovering a large oak door. They then drilled a series of holes around the lock and using a reciprocating saw they cut around the lock. Finally, it was removed.

'Quick, we need to get her out,' shouted Jane.

'Wait, Jane, I know you're desperate to see whether Lara is OK, but we have to tread carefully. She's been alone and in darkness for a long time. If we go rushing in she will be terrified. I'll go in first.'

The senior policeman entered the chamber.

'Hello, Lara. This is the police. We're here to rescue you. Lara, can you hear me?'

He stepped further into the chamber. He could just see a stretcher against the wall and in the dim light of his torch he could see Lara covered by a blanket.

'Lara, can you hear me?'

There was no reply.

He approached the gaunt figure. She was unconscious. He held her wrist to check for a pulse – she was alive, but the pulse was very weak.

The Inspector left the chamber to organise Lara's removal from the chamber.

'She's alive, but unconscious. Her pulse is weak. We need the ambulance officers here quickly.'

'They have already arrived, sir.'

'Excellent, get them to take her out immediately.'

Two ambulance officers entered the chamber and checked Lara's vital signs. Her body temperature, pulse rate, respiration rate and blood pressure were all at critical levels. The two officers carefully lifted Lara onto a gurney and wheeled her out into the medieval tunnel.

Jane approached Lara kissing her hand and telling her how much she loved her.

Lara was placed in an ambulance and then transferred to Kelso Hospital where her recovery process would begin.

'Thank you, Jane. Without you Lara would have died,' said the Chief Inspector.

'I'm just glad I could help. I just pray Lara will be OK.'

'Only time and the right medical treatment will determine that.'

Jane was prohibited from visiting her friend for the first few days, although she spent many hours in the visitors' waiting room.

One of Lara's doctors kept Jane informed of her friend's progress. He explained what had happened to Lara's body through lack of food.

'The rough part occurs after 72 hours of no eating – this is the stage of autophagy. Once the fats are broken down, the body turns to breaking down protein in muscles, essentially wasting away Lara's muscles. At this point, her brain's requirement for glucose would have dropped from 120 grams per day to only 30 grams. But, her brain still needed energy from protein. Breaking down protein and releasing amino acids into the bloodstream produced more glucose. This transformation takes place in the liver, and Lara's brain was fuelled by its much-needed glucose once again. Regardless, her brain was able to survive from using up protein, but her muscles have deteriorated.

'Interestingly, the greatest amount of protein loss occurs during the first 72 hours. Afterwards, the body adapts to conserve protein. Primarily, Lara's metabolism slowed down so much, to the point that her body used the smallest amount of energy possible.'

'So Doctor, Lara hasn't suffered any brain damage has she?'

'We don't believe so, but it's still too early to say conclusively.'

'When will I be able to see her?'

'Maybe tomorrow.'

'Thank you doctor.'

TRUST, BUT VERIFY.

RONALD REAGAN

CHAPTER 16

The medical team at Kelso Hospital was pleased with Lara's recovery. Her physical health was near normal after two weeks in care but they were concerned about her mental state.

What Lara had experienced in captivity had resulted in her contracting Post Traumatic Stress Disorder. If left untreated she could fall into a deep depression.

Both Lisbeth and Jane were deeply concerned. Lara refused to leave Westmoreland and felt very uncomfortable if she wasn't in the company of one of the two women.

Jane had to return to America to continue her postgraduate university studies but was reluctant to leave Lara. Lisbeth assured her it would be OK.

She was referred to one of the best psychiatrists in Britain, R D Laing; he took Lara's case after reading about her kidnapping.

For the following six months Lara would visit Dr Laing, Lisbeth drove her to Edinburgh and waited for her then drove her back. Over this period Lisbeth began to notice an improvement in Lara's attitude culminating in Lara suggesting that she and Lisbeth go to the movies to see *The Spy Who Came in From the Cold* with Richard Burton and Clair Bloom.

'Lara, that would be wonderful darling. But why that particular movie? I believe *Sound of Music* is excellent.'

'I read the book some time ago. I'd like to see it.'

'Well then, so we shall. When would you like to go?'

'How about tomorrow?'

'Why not?'

Lisbeth was delighted that Lara felt confident enough to venture out in the outside world. The two women drove into Edinburgh where the film was being shown. Lisbeth parked the Mini however Lara was not making any effort to get out of the car.

'Are you OK, Lara?'

'Not really. I think I'm having a panic attack. Dr Laing warned me I could suffer from them.'

'Why don't I come around and help you out.'

'Alright, will you hold my hand?'

'Of course, I will darling.'

They walked hand in hand. Lisbeth purchased the tickets but upon entering the darkened theatre Lara stopped.

'I can't.'

'It's OK darling I'm right beside you.' Lisbeth found their seats.

Darkness was difficult for Lara. She slept with a light on since experiencing the blackness for days on end in her prison. They sat in their seats just as the movie began and Lara was so enraptured in the film that she forgot the darkness. It turned out to be a turning point for Lara's recovery and re-entry into everyday life.

Lara spent most of her time riding her new horse, Sultan, around the estate, however, she didn't venture anywhere near where Megan's accident occurred. She also began to drive again but didn't venture far, mostly to the local village Gairloch.

1966

David Bowie releases the first record 'Can't Help Thinking About Me'

Indira Gandhi elected India's fourth President

Syrian military coup takes place under Hafiz al-Assad

June 1966

Lara decided it was time to return to Westmoreland. She knew she would never go back to Raby Castle again and thought long and hard as to what to do. It was while she was riding Sultan that an idea came to her. She would donate a 25-year lease to Edinburgh University Medical School. Lara knew it would be wrong to transfer the title for the castle as it had been in her family for centuries, but a renewable lease would serve her purpose. She would request the school be named after her mother and father. It became 'The Harold and Julie de Neville School of Medicine.' She decided not to use their titles – that would be too formal.

She contacted Sir Horace who still acted as her solicitor. He agreed it was a splendid idea, although he warned her that she would decrease her income by a considerable amount and suggested the farm income be retained. She thought about it for some time before finally deciding to lease the castle on five acres of land and continue to have the estate worked by the existing staff. This would serve two purposes: income and ensuring that loyal employees retained their jobs.

Lara decided to keep all the furniture and the artwork including the family portraits dating back 400 years and have them stored in Edinburgh.

On further reflection, she decided that the artwork would be kept in storage however she decided to auction the furniture – not in London but in Scotland, so that the local people would have a chance to purchase a piece of history.

A team of workers was organised to clear the castle, taking a month to do so. The day of the auction came.

September 1964

The auction was held in the great hall in Raby Castle. It attracted a large crowd eager to pick up an antique at a bargain price.

By the end of the day, 80 per cent of the lots had sold and the remaining lots would be purchased privately.

Brian McCollum had his eye on a beautiful chest of drawers and made an offer of £70. It was accepted and he arranged for his son and a mate to load it on the back of Brian's truck.

Brian, his wife and son, lived on a small farm in Penicuik District not far from Raby Castle. They raised pigs, chickens and milked a small herd of dairy cows. The family was not wealthy, but they were not regarded as poor.

When Brian arrived home with a 17th-century fine oak chest of drawers his wife, Mary was astounded.

'What are you going to do with that?'

'Darling, it's beautiful. It's an antique from Raby Castle.'

'How much did you pay for it?'

'Only 70 quid. It was a real bargain.'

'Well, I'm glad you've got 70 quid to waste on a fancy chest of drawers we don't need.'

Mary stormed off into the farmhouse leaving Billy, her son and his mate Rob to help Brian unload the chest of drawers.

'Where are you going to put it, Dad?'

'I think we'll put it in the shed Billy. I'll polish it up and get it looking grand. When your mum next sees it, she'll love it.'

The three men carried the heavy piece of furniture into the machinery shed.

Brian spent all his spare time polishing the wood and the brass handles, hoping Mary would accept the fine piece of furniture into their house.

Brian was on his knees polishing the base of the chest of drawers when he noticed a slight indentation in the side of the piece. He pushed the depression, revealing a secret compartment. Inside it was a sports bag. Brian retrieved the bag, unzipped it and peered inside.

He wasn't sure, but thought he might have discovered the missing diamonds that Lord de Neville had demanded as a ransom to release the young Countess de Neville. Everybody in Britain knew about the missing £5,000,000 in uncut diamonds.

Brian carried the bag into the farmhouse and showed his wife.

'They just look like glass to me love. Are you sure they're the missing diamonds?'

'Well, you think about Mary. A bag in a secret compartment located in an antique chest of drawers which came from Raby Castle. I don't think anyone would bother to hide glass stones.'

'So what do you think we should do with them?' asked Brian.

'Well, I think there's only one thing we can do. Take them to the police.'

'So you don't believe that we should keep a few?'

'I'm sure it's very well documented how many diamonds there was love.'

'Yeah, you're right darling. We better do the right thing.'

Brian and his son Billy drove to the village of Gairloch parking outside the village police station. Walking inside, Brian placed the heavy bag on the counter.

'I'd like to speak to the senior officer in charge please.'

'Would you? And why is that?' asked the young constable manning the front desk.

'I believe I've found the missing diamonds from the Raby Castle kidnapping.'

The police officer immediately contacted his superior via the office intercom. Within a minute, the sergeant came to the desk and invited Brian into his office. The farmer explained how he had found the bag and where he had purchased the chest of drawers.

Sergeant McDonald looked inside the bag, but knowing very little about diamonds he was undecided as to their authenticity.

'I'll contact Chief Inspector Russell at Scotland Yard. He was the officer in charge of the investigation. I would imagine he would organise the safe transportation of the bag to London. I will sign a receipt for the goods, which I would suggest you keep in a safe place. Thank you for your honesty, Mr McCollum. It's not every day we get £5,000,000 in uncut diamonds handed over at the front desk.'

The Chief Inspector was excited by the prospect of recovering Lara's ransom. He drove to Scotland with a police escort to collect the diamonds and transport them back to London.

Once the diamonds were verified by De Beers, they were handed over to the de Neville estate. The diamond trader agreed to take back the diamonds and transfer £5,000,000 to Lara's bank account.

Brian was feeding the pigs when he saw a Rolls Royce making its way up the dirt driveway.

'Who the fuck is this?' he thought.

A rather large pompous-looking gentleman got out of the back.

'Good afternoon. My name is Sir Horace Winterbottom. I take it you are Mr Brian McCollum?'

'Yeah, that's right, what can I do for you?'

'I represent the Countess de Neville, formerly of Raby Castle.'

'Oh right, the one that got kidnapped. I found the ransom did you know that?'

'Indeed I did Mr McCollum. That's the reason for my visit. The Countess was grateful for your honesty and has asked me to pay you a reward.'

'Oh yeah? That's nice. How much?'

Sir Horace passed Brian an envelope. He opened it and looked at the cheque it contained.

'Holy hell! £100,000! I don't believe it. You'll have to excuse me, Sir Horace. I've got to tell Mary.'

Brian raced over to the house, yelling out to his wife. He showed her the cheque made out to the both of them. They both began to cry they knew that this would change their lives.

FLOWER POWER

CHAPTER 17

1966

Mohammad Ali becomes world heavy weight champion

Nelson Mandala sentenced to life in prison

Beatles conquer the USA

Lara completed her medical degree at Oxford with distinctions in the December of 1966. Some hospitals in and around London offered her an internship, but she was still intent on visiting Jane in San Francisco. The young medical graduate was sitting in the conservatory at Westmoreland reading the latest *OZ* magazine. She found it rude, crude and very amusing.

She heard the telephone ring inside the house. A servant answered it and came out to the conservatory.

'Lara, there's a Miss Jane calling from America. Would you like to take the call?'

Lara insisted that the staff address her by the first name. She didn't like the formality of Ma'am.

'Yes, I do thank you.'

The servant, Beverley handed the telephone to her mistress, making sure the long cord did not become entangled.

'Hello darling! How are you?'

'I'm fantastic Lars. I'm having a great time here. You know the house I bought a while back? Well, guess who's my next door neighbour?'

'I have no idea. Who?'

'Janis Joplin.'

'You're kidding me! Have you met her yet?'

'Absolutely! She comes over for a drink quite often.'

'I thought you would have shared a joint.'

'No, Janis doesn't do drugs anymore. When she first arrived in San Francisco she got caught up in the drug scene. She was shooting up speed apparently, it nearly killed her. She went back to Texas for a year, and her family got her back on the straight and narrow.'

'Straight and narrow is not a term I would have associated with Janis Joplin.'

'Hey, don't get me wrong. She's no princess. She drinks copious amounts of bourbon and leads a pretty wild life. Having said that, she's great, just a regular girl like us. She promised me she'd introduce me to a few of her muso friends.'

'Yeah like, who?'

'Like, Jerry Garcia.'

'From the Grateful Dead? I don't believe it! They're one of my favourite bands.'

'Not only that. Guess who her best friend is? Grace Slick.'

'Jefferson Airplane – another favourite.'

'Sweetheart, you've got to get your pretty ass over here and feel the vibe. The Hippy scene has taken over San Francisco. I live in Ashbury Street about half a mile from the intersection of Haight and Ashbury, the centre of where it's all happening.

Grateful Dead

'You can stay with me for as long as you like.'

'Are you working Jane? You were going to join some old established law firm?'

'I'm not a Hippy Lara! Yes, I joined Orrick & Co, and I love it. It's just great living in this part of the world – the people the music and the grass isn't bad either.'

'Ok, darling. I'll check with the airlines. I need to ensure all is well here too. I'm sure Lisbeth will look after things for me while I'm gone.'

'I can't wait to see you, Lars.'

'Me neither, Jane.'

Lara organised her personal affairs and ensured Lisbeth was happy to continue to run the Westmoreland household. Lara paid her a very considerable income, not just for her services but for the support she had given Lara since she was six years old.

1967

Donald Campbell killed driving the Bluebird Jet boat trying to break his own water speed record

Edward Brooke became the first African American to be elected to the US Senate

Rolling Stones released *Lets Spend the Night Together*

1 January 1967

Once all was in order, the Countess de Neville flew to San Francisco. Her closest friend was at the airport to welcome her.

'Hey you, welcome to San Francisco.'

'Hi Jane, it's great to be here.'

'Are you ready for the grand tour?'

'Actually, I'm ready for a sleep.'

'No, they say the best way to get over jet lag is to carry on as usual and sleep at your regular time.'

'Who the hell are 'they' and what would they know anyway?'

'Come on babe, we'll go home via the city centre so you can get a feel for the place, and then we'll head home via Golden Gate Park. You'll love it.'

'OK, let's go.'

The two friends headed for the car park, finding Jane's transport on level three.

'Wow Jane! You really have gotten into this hippie thing. This is magic. Did you buy it like this or did you get it painted?'

'I bought it like this. I saw Janis's Porsche and got inspired.'

'My God! What's her Porsche like?'

'You'll see when we get home. She parks it on the street outside her house.'

Jane and Lara drove through the CBD, which the English girl liked. Union Square stood out. Lara couldn't get over the steepness of the streets and how the cable cars climbed them with relative ease.

As Jane made her way to Golden Gate Park, Lara was excited to see the famous bridge plus Alcatraz island not that far off shore as they drove along the bay foreshore.

She drove through the Park, which Lara enjoyed. Although not as large as Hyde Park back home the different trees and shrubs made it interesting.

'Right, we're almost home. Just a couple of minutes.'

Once they reached the Haight-Ashbury area, it was only a short distance to Ashbury Street where Jane lived. Driving up Haight Street Lara saw hippie guys and girls everywhere – some had flowers in their hair, and most of them were dressed in colourful clothes that looked like they hadn't been washed for a good six months; neither had their hair.

The Kombi Van turned into Ashbury Street and right in front of them was Jane's neighbour, Janis Joplin, in her Porsche.

Jane stopped the Kombi to have a brief chat. She introduced Lara and suggested to Janis she pop in after dinner.

'Sure, I'd love to Jane. I'll bring a bottle of *Southern Comfort.*'

Janis drove off at speed as she normally did. She could afford the speeding fines which was just as well as she seemed to get them with monotonous regularity.

'She's probably off to the liquor store to buy the *Southern Comfort,*' said Lara.

'Unlikely. She'd have dozens stored at her house. She probably drinks a bottle a day.'

'My goodness! Is she an alcoholic?'

'I don't know. Probably.'

Jane parked the psychedelic Kombi outside her house 633 Ashbury Street.

Jane, it's beautiful. Unique architecture, I must say. I can't wait to see inside.'

The two friends took Lara's luggage into the magnificent 'Painted Lady' as these San Francisco houses were called. The décor was reminiscent of a Hindu temple and Lara was fascinated. It was an entirely different style than the old English she was used to.

Jane's Living Room

Jane showed her the guest room which also followed the eastern theme.

'Darling, it's beautiful. You'll never get rid of me.'

'As I said earlier, you're welcome to stay as long as you like.'

'I know I suggested you stay awake until your usual bedtime, but maybe a nap for an hour could do you the world of good. While you have some shut-eye, I'll prepare dinner.'

'That sounds like a fantastic idea, babe. Thanks.'

Jane prepared a vegetarian lasagne and salad; she had a couple of bottles of white wine in the fridge as an accompaniment.

At six pm Jane went up to Lara's room and knocked. There was no reply. She gently opened the bedroom door to find her friend moaning and thrashing about in the bed.

'My God, she's having a fit,' thought Jane.

She quickly went over to the bed and held her friend's hand. Lara opened her eyes and stared back blankly.

'Oh God! I'm sorry Jane. I must have scared the living daylights out of you. I still have horrible nightmares about the kidnapping.'

'Oh, you poor baby! Don't worry you're safe here with me. Why don't you have a shower and freshen up? Then we can have dinner.'

Jane set the table and waited for her houseguest to come downstairs to join her. Lara felt better having showered and changed her clothes. The only outfit she had that resembled hippie was an Indian kaftan.

'Darling you look like you've been living in Haight-Ashbury forever. I love your outfit.'

'Well, I thought I should try and fit in with the scene as they say.'

'You do. I don't think a twin set and bobby socks would impress Janis. Would you like a glass of white wine?'

'I'd love one, thank you.'

'Would you mind if I asked you if the police ever discovered why Andrew did such a horrid thing?'

Lara recounted what she knew about the Ponzi scheme and how Andrew lost all his wealth.

'I'm afraid it was an act of desperation. I honestly didn't think he wanted to hurt me. It was his death that caused me to suffer so much locked away in that black hole.'

'It must have been horrible. Now that's enough of that! On a lighter note we need to plan what we're going to do for the next couple of weeks. I have taken the time off work so we can play the tourist as much as we like.'

'I would love you to drive me across the Golden Gate Bridge in the Kombi. And I want to see the giant redwoods while we are on the other side of the bay.'

'OK, that's a good start. Anything else?'

'I naturally want to go down to the piers and feed the seagulls.'

'That can be arranged. We might even feed ourselves down there – the restaurants serve fantastic clam chowder.'

The doorbell rang. Jane welcomed Janis, inviting her to join them in the living room. As promised, she had a bottle of *Southern Comfort* with her.

'Ladies I've got some news. *Down on Me* has gone to number 42 just two more fucking slots to go and it's a top 40 hit.'

'That's great, Janis. I'm sure it will reach 40 and better,' said Jane.

'It's surely worth drinking to.'

'Would you like a glass, babe?'

'Don't be silly, you know I drink from the bottle. A glass is a useless piece of apparatus as far as I'm concerned.'

'So, Lara ... it is Lara isn't it? What brings you to our fair city of love and peace?'

'Just that, love and peace. I certainly could use some.'

'Yeah, couldn't we all sweetheart? So you're from England I take it?'

'That's right.'

'I've never been there, but it is surely my intention. I keep on about it with our manager Julius, but he hasn't been able to organise anything yet.'

'You should go, Janis, you'd enjoy the scene there. So many great bands are located in the UK.'

'Yeah, I know a good friend of mine Jimmie Hendrix is over there now. He loves it. Mind you, I'm not sure if he loves the music or the women more – he's a wild boy.'

'Jane baby what are you going to do with Lara while she's here?'

'We've got some plans, but nothing too exhausting. You know the standard touristy things.'

'Are you going to the 'Human Be-In' at Golden Gate Park on January 14?'

'I thought about it. But I believe that it might be too much for Lara to handle. They say there could be up to 30,000 people going.'

'You can't miss out on the greatest event of the century. You must go –after all I'll be singing.

'I'll get you into the VIP area. You won't have to compete with the masses. Anybody who's anybody will be playing including The Mamas and the Poppas, The Grateful Dead, Jefferson Airplane – everybody. I can introduce you.'

'What do you think, Lara?'

'Are you kidding? I'd love to go.'

'Right, that's settled. I'll drop in the VIP passes in a few days. OK, I'd better go and get some beauty sleep. Let's catch up soon.'

'I can't believe it. I'm going to meet some of the greatest artists in the world,' said Lara.

'I told you you'd love it here.'

The two friends played the tourist over the following days. The highlight for Lara was walking among the giant redwoods.

Giant Redwood

TURN ON, TUNE IN, DROP OUT

TIMOTHY LEARY

CHAPTER 18

14 January arrived and Janis dropped in the VIP passes the day before, as promised. Not only would they be in a separate area close to the stage but they would enter the park using the same gate as the artists and speakers, such as Dr Timothy Leary and Allan Ginsberg.

The day was perfect: blue sky with a gentle breeze coming from the bay and people were filling the vast grass area of the polo ground. It looked like the forecasted numbers were proving to be accurate.

The first act to blow everybody away was Grateful Dead followed by Quicksilver Messenger, Jefferson Airplane, Big Brother Holding Company and many more bands.

Grateful Dead

Jefferson Airplane

Janis Joplin & Big Brother and the Holding Company

The organisers promised one million LSD tabs would be given away. Judging by the behaviour of a large section of the crowd many took advantage. The sound of the bands permeated to the very edge of the field; hippies were dancing slowly and the smell of marijuana wafted over the crowd. It was a very primaeval scene.

Jane and Lara were offered LSD but declined. They did accept a joint to share which had a similar effect and they too danced in a slow rhythmic fashion.

'How good was Janis? That girl's got a voice,' said Jane.

'I hope she comes in here,' said Lara

'Don't worry, she said she would.'

'There she is! Janis over here, babe,' shouted Jane.

'Hey, how are you ladies enjoying yourselves?'

'Unbelievable! I've never seen or heard anything like it. I thought the Beatles concert was fantastic, but this tops it,' said Jane.

'You've seen the Beatles?'

'Yeah, in London when I was living over there.'

'I didn't know you'd lived in England.'

'Yeah, that's where I met Lara. My parents moved there when I was young.'

'What about you, Lara? Enjoying yourself?'

'I'm blown away by it all Janis, Your performance was unbelievable.'

'Why thank you, babe.'

'So what are you doing after the gig?' asked Jane.

'A few of us are going back to my place – you're welcome to come.'

'That would be great. What time?'

'Get there about 8 pm.'

The two apprentice hippies made their way back through the throng. Jane thanked her lucky stars that she was able to park the Kombi in the performer's car park; returning home wasn't a major drama.

They had a bite to eat and rested up until it was time to go next door. They heard people arriving and figured they should go. Jane knocked on the brightly painted door – it was opened by Jerry Garcia.

'Hi, ladies. I'm Jerry. Come on in, I take it you know Janis?'

'We live next door. I'm Jane and this is my friend Lara.'

'Janis is out the back. Just go through. She'll be pleased to see you.'

The two girls made their way to the back of the house where Janis was holding court on the back deck.

'Can you believe it? Jerry Garcia opens the door for us,' whispered Lara.

'Hey girls, I'm glad you could make it. Come over, and I'll introduce you around.

'This is Grace. She sings with Jefferson Airplane.'

'As if I didn't know that,' thought Lara.

'And this is Skip. He plays the drums with the group.'

'Go and get yourselves a drink and come back.'

The two star-struck women went back into the house to pour themselves a glass. Standing at the drinks table was a good-looking young man with long blonde hair, wearing a colourful vest, jeans and cowboy boots.

'Can I help you, ladies, what would you like to drink?'

'Yes, thank you. I'd like a white wine what about you, Lara?'

'I might have a *Southern Comfort* and *Coke* please.'

'Ah, the poison of choice in this household.'

'So, I detect an English accent. Where in Britain are you from?'

'A place called Somerset. You probably haven't heard of it.'

'I've been to Bath. That's in Somerset, isn't it?'

'Yes, you're quite right. When were you there?'

'About three years ago my parents took my sister Anna and me on the grand tour of Europe.'

'What's your name by the way?' asked Lara.

'David.'

'And yours?'

'Lara.'

'Which band do you play with?'

'I'm not a musician. I'm just a roadie.'

'Excuse my ignorance, but what's a roadie?'

'I unload all the gear and then pack it up at the end of the gig. Not very glamorous I'm afraid.'

'Well, you'd get to see a lot of free concerts. Which band do you work for?'

'Big Brother and the Holding Company.'

'So that's why you're here?'

Yeah. I knew Janis at high School. She's the one who talked me into working for her band.

'What high school?'

'Thomas Jefferson in Port Arthur, Texas.'

'I've not heard of it.'

'Port Arthur is not much of a town. It only exists to service a large oil refinery.'

'So what brought you to San Francisco?'

'Initially I came here to attend the University of California.'

'To study what?'

'Medicine.'

'How far did you get?'

'I feel like I'm being interviewed.'

'Oh, I'm sorry. I only ask because I'm interested.'

'It's OK. I passed the third year, which means I have another two years to go.'

'Do you think you'll go back?'

'I think so. I'm keen to graduate and do my internship then continue further studies to specialise in plastic surgery.'

'That's amazing.'

'What's amazing?'

'I have just completed my medical degree at Oxford. I also intend to specialise in plastic surgery. Both my parents were plastic surgeons.'

'Fantastic! So you'll be joining the family business no doubt.'

'No, they are both dead, I'm afraid.'

'Oh, I am sorry.'

'Don't be. They both died when I was six. So why did you drop out? Did Timothy Leary have anything to do with it?'

'No, I just saw what was happening around Haight-Ashbury and wanted to be part of it. I always knew I would return to medical school.'

'Well, David, I better try and find Jane. It's been very nice talking to you.'

Lara wandered through the house looking for her friend. She found her sitting on a couch talking to Grace Slick.

'Hi Lars come and join us.'

'Hello Lara,' said Grace.

'We've been talking about how the music scene is constantly changing in San Francisco.'

'I'm sorry, but I have just arrived in America and not up with the US music scene. Having said that Grace, you and the band, were fantastic today.'

'Thank you, Lara, I'm glad you enjoyed our gig.'

'Will you both excuse me? I want to catch David before the end of the night.'

'Not at all. Who's David?

'He's the guy that served us our drink.'

'Go for it, babe.'

Lara headed back to the front of the house where she last saw the roadie. She was keen to get to know him better, much better. He was no longer at the drinks table nor the sitting room where they had their conversation. She moved from room to room, but it was obvious David was no longer there.

Disappointed, Lara returned to the deck. Janis approached her.

'Lara, it seems you've made quite an impression on our roadie.'

'Did I, how do you know Janis?'

'He told me. Don't be surprised if he calls you.'

'I didn't give him Jane's number.'

'I did. I hope that's OK with you?'

'Yes, of course, I was very impressed with him.'

'Impressed. Now that's good.'

'So I take it he's left for the night?'

'Yeah, he had to check the gear for tomorrow night's gig.'

At 1 am Jane and Lara decided it was time to go home, not that they had far to go. They bid each other goodnight and retired to their respective bedrooms.

Next morning over breakfast Jane brought up the subject of David.

'So, you fox! I understand you have a suitor?'

'I wouldn't say that.'

'Well, Janis tells me he intends to call you and ask you out.'

'We'll see.'

The telephone rang. Jane answered.

'Hi, it's David Benson. Is Lara home?'

'I'll just go and check David, hold the line.'

'Are you home?'

'Of course I'm home. Hand over the phone.'

'Hello, this is Lara.'

'Hi Lara, it's David. I was talking to you last night at Janis's place.'

'Yes, I remember. How are you?'

'I'm good, although I didn't get to bed until 4 am.'

'My God, why not?'

'I had to take all the sound gear over to Fillmore West. There's a big concert there tonight, and it was the only time we had access.'

'So Janis and the boys are playing?'

'Yeah and the Grateful Dead, plus the Mamas and Papas and a new guy who's a buddy of John Phillips called Scott McKenzie. Apparently, John wrote him a song, which he sings for the first time tonight. It sounds cool. It's called 'If You're Going to San Francisco.'

'It sounds as if it will be a great concert.'

'Well, that's the reason I rang. Would you like to go? I can organise VIP seats.'

'I'd love to David. What time?'

'Let's say I pick you up at 7 pm.'

'I'm looking forward to it.'

'Great, we can grab a bite after the concert.'

'Sounds good. See you tonight.'

'OK. Bye, Lara.'

Lara hung up the telephone and smiled at her friend.

'So, what's happening girlfriend?'

'He's asked me out to a concert tonight and then dinner.'

'That sounds promising. You like him don't you?'

'I do. He's attractive and quite intelligent.'

'Not to mention good-looking with a body to match.'

'Well, that doesn't hurt.'

The two friends decided to catch a bus to Union Square so Lara could buy a new outfit. She found something suitable at Macys. It was a hippie designer outfit, a step up from what she could have purchased at Haight-Ashbury.

Once they arrived home, Lara showered and got ready for her date to pick her up at 7 pm.

Right on time, there was a knock on the front door. Jane answered it showing David into the living room. Ten minutes later Lara appeared.

'Wow, you look stunning Lara.'

'Thank you.'

'Right, shall we go?'

'OK, bye Jane,'

'Bye, you two have a great night.'

'I hope you don't mind I'm driving the band's van. I cleaned it up as best I could.'

'No that's fine, David.'

The roadie drove the van the ten minutes to Fillmore West, parking the van at the back of the venue.

Fillmore West

'We'll enter through the stage door. Saves queuing up out the front.'

Lara and David climbed the back stairs. He unlocked the stage door, and they both entered. Lara was presented with a scene of organised chaos.

People were moving sound equipment onto the stage, tuning guitars and assembling drum kits, all with just twenty minutes to go before the first act, The Big Brother Holding Company.

'Why don't we go and see Janis and the boys? I want to make sure they're happy with the way things have been set up.'

They walked down a corridor until they reached the dressing room for the band. David knocked. A woman's voice responded.

'Come in if you're good looking.'

Dave Getz, the drummer, opened the door.

'Hey, Dave and Lara! How the fuck are you?' asked Janis.

'We're good. Are you ready to blow them away?'

'Of course.'

'I've done the sound check, and it's all good. You're on in ten minutes.'

'Excellent! Gives time for one more drink.'

'OK well, we'll be in the VIP section screaming for more.'

'Will we see you after the show?'

'Lara and I are going out for dinner. We'll have to take a rain check.'

'So you're on a date?'

'I suppose we are.'

'I'll see you both soon. Don't do anything I wouldn't do.'

David thought to himself, 'as if '.

They left the dressing room and began making their way to the theatre. John and Michelle Phillips from The Mamas and Papas passed them in the corridor; Lara couldn't believe it.

David and Lara made their way down to the VIP seats where they had a perfect view of the stage. They didn't have to wait long. Big Brother, and the Holding Company was announced and Janis and the band started their session with *Down on Me*. This was followed up with *Easy Rider*, *Woman is Losers*, *All is Loneliness* and *Blind Man*.

The crowd went ballistic – for many it was the first time they had heard Janis Joplin sing.

Janis Joplin

The Mamas and Papas followed opening with Dedicated to the One I Love then Creeque Alley, Monday, Monday and finishing with Dancing in the Street.

Mamas and Papas

John Phillips introduced Scott McKenzie and the song he wrote for Scott *If You're Going to San Francisco*. The audience loved it.

Scott McKenzie

The final act was the Grateful Dead. This was the band most of the audience came to see. They opened with *The Golden Road* followed by *Beat it Down the Line*, *Good Morning Little School Girl*, *Cold Rain and Snow*, *Sitting on Top of the World* and closed with *Viola Lee Blues*.

Grateful Dead

David and Lara agreed it was the best concert they had been to which was remarkable seeing as David attended two or more concerts a week. It might have resulted from the fact they were both attracted to each other and enjoyed each other's company – the concert may have been secondary.

'How hungry are you, Lara?'

'I'm not starving, but I wouldn't mind something light to eat.'

'OK, why don't we go down to The Drug Store Café. They serve great pizzas.'

'That sounds good to me.'

SUMMER OF LOVE

CHAPTER 19

May 1967

David and Lara became an item. Lara would attend concerts but not all of them. She needed some time to herself. She became close to Janis, and Grace. The young countess from England found their attitudes and way of life uplifting. Both singers didn't take crap from anybody; an attribute Lara admired.

Lara was contemplating extending her stay in America. She was enjoying the Californian lifestyle, and she had fallen in love with David. To leave now seemed unthinkable.

After careful consideration, she decided to contact the John Hopkins Hospital to determine if they would accept her as an intern. Her application was approved – after all she was a Margaret Harris Memorial Prize winner at Oxford.

The other important decision she made was to purchase a house not far from the Haight-Ashbury precinct, a beautiful house at 630 Page Street within walking distance of Jane's and Janis's homes.

630 Page Street

Lara was hoping David would agree to move in with her but the conundrum she now faced was how to explain how she could afford such a house. She had not divulged her past to him, not all of it anyway. She had to decide how much she revealed, including the extent of her wealth. The only person who knew of her peerage and wealth was Jane and she was sworn to secrecy. She decided just to get on with it. She telephoned him.

'Hi babe, I was wondering if you could meet me somewhere I have something to show you.'

'That sounds kind of mysterious. Where do you want to meet?'

'Have you got a pen? Write down this address: 630 Page Street Lower Haight.'

'Are you going to tell me why?'

'Just meet me there and all will be revealed. Can you be there at 5 pm tonight?'

'Yeah, that should be OK. See you then.'

The other significant decision Lara made was to purchase a Kombi Camper. She had ambitions to visit some national parks such as Yosemite and Yellowstone. The car was being delivered to Jane's house that afternoon at three.

Soon after 3 pm, a brand new Kombi Camper parked outside Jane's house; it was bright red and white and it looked stunning. The driver knocked on the front door Lara answered it.

'I have a delivery for Miss de Neville.'

'Yes, that's me.'

'Well, miss I believe payment has been made so the only thing you need from me is a demonstration as to how everything works.'

The man from the Volkswagen dealer showed Lara how the various components worked, including the pop-up roof. He gave her the keys and wished her well. A colleague from the showroom drove him back.

Jane came out to inspect the new car.

'Hey, Lars you'll have to get the psychedelic paint job on it like mine.'

'I'm afraid not. This baby is going cruising through the national parks. Crazy paint wouldn't suit the image.

'Come on, take me for a spin.'

The two friends drove through Haight-Ashbury and into Golden Gate Park and returned to Ashbury Street.

'Drives like a dream, babe. And you've got a bed in the back so you can get laid wherever you happen to be.'

'Speaking of getting laid, I'm meeting David at the house at 5. I'll take the Kombi. That should totally blow him away.'

David was curious: Why had Lara asked him to meet her at an unfamiliar address? He drove the van to 630 Page Street in Lower Haight. Outside the beautiful Victorian house was a new VW Kombi Camper.

'So this is what she wanted to show me. Nice rig,' he thought.

David got out of the van and examined the new Kombi.

'No way this is Lara's. Must be someone else's living on the street.'

The front door of number 630 opened. Lara was standing on the threshold and beckoned David into the amazing house.

'Hi, babe whose house?'

'Mine. Come on in.'

'Yours? How in the hell?'

'Come inside and I'll tell you.'

The proud new house owner showed her boyfriend through the 5-bedroom Victorian home. It had no furniture as yet. That was a task she hoped David would help her with. Choosing the right furniture was important.

'Its beautiful Lara, But you still haven't explained to me how you were able to afford such a magnificent place. You could tell me it's none of my business.'

'Don't be silly, babe! It is your business. I've told you that both my parents were killed in a boating accident on the Chesapeake Bay in 1948.'

'Yes, tragic.'

'Well I was their only child. They left me some money which has accumulated over the years hence being able to purchase this house and the Kombi Camper out front.'

'The Kombi's yours as well?'

'Yes, beautiful isn't it?'

'Wow, you have blown me way, Lars.'

'Well, here's something else, babe. How would you like to move in?'

'What, move in with you?'

'Only if you want to.'

'Yes I'd love to. Are you sure you want to do this?'

'I wouldn't have asked you if I wasn't sure.'

'I'm trying to get my head round this but what I do know Lara is that I love you.'

'I love you too David.'

David moved out of his shared house in Haight-Ashbury, bidding farewell to his seven housemates. He only had his clothes and an old guitar given to him by James Gurley, the lead guitarist of the group.

He and Lara headed out to buy some furniture. They were able to furnish most of the house from Funky Furniture in Lissom @ 7th. They purchased a fridge and a television set elsewhere, and they were ready to move in.

The lovebirds were sitting in the courtyard enjoying a *Southern Comfort* and *Coke* discussing their plans. Lara was due to begin her internship on 1st July, which was only four weeks away. They both knew her spare time would be limited as the workload of an intern in a major hospital was intense. They also discussed David's ambition to return to medical school to complete his degree. They both decided that he should re-enrol, beginning his fourth year the following January.

'Hey, babe I'm obligated to go to the Monterey Pop Festival to roadie for the group. It's going to be the biggest and best festival ever. Why don't we both go?'

'Yeah, we could take the Kombi. That would take care of the accommodation.'

'Great it starts on June 16 and ends on the 18th.'

'So who's playing?'

'Yes, they are.'

'Beg your pardon.'

'Sorry, just kidding! The Who are one of the bands playing.'

'Come on, which bands are playing?'

'I've got the playlist here. Take a look.'

Friday, June 16, 1967

Beverley Martyn

Eric Burdon & the Animals

Johnny Rivers

Lou Rawls

Simon & Garfunkel

The Association

The Paupers

Saturday, June 17, 1967

Al Kooper

Big Brother & The Holding Company

Booker T. & The MG's

Canned Heat

Country Joe and the Fish

Hugh Masekela

Jefferson Airplane

Laura Nyro

Moby Grape

Otis Redding

Quicksilver Messenger Service

Steve Miller Band

The Byrds

The Electric Flag

The Paul Butterfield Blues Band

Sunday, June 18, 1967

Big Brother & The Holding Company

Buffalo Springfield

Cyrus Faryar

Grateful Dead

Ravi Shankar

The Blues Project

The Jimi Hendrix Experience

The Mamas & the Papas

The Who

'Unbelievable! What a lineup! Pity the Beatles aren't playing.'

'Apparently Paul McCartney was at Mama Cass's house with John and Michelle Phillips when they all came up with the idea for the festival.'

'So why aren't the Beatles headlining?'

'Their music has become too complex to play live, is the supposed reason.'

'And what about the Rolling Stones?'

'I don't know why they're not playing. But I heard Brian Jones would be there.'

'Well, it's a huge line-up. It'll be fun.'

MONTEREY

CHAPTER 20

Friday 16 June 1967

Lara and David started their road trip to Monterey at 8 am trying to beat the traffic. Unfortunately, many others had the same thought and instead of taking two hours it ended up a four-hour journey. David knew the road well because he had driven the band's gear to Monterey the day before, and that trip only took two and a half hours.

Once they reached the fairgrounds, they used the pass to park the Kombi in the entertainers' car park where many artists were camped in Winnebagos, caravans, even tents.

David found a suitable parking spot not too far from the amenities. Once set up they decided to take a walk and check out the stage and the venue itself.

As they strolled through the grounds, they bumped into Grace Slick, who greeted them both affectionately.

'Hi, you guys, is this going to be unbelievable or what?'

'With the bands playing how could it not,' said Lara.

'No doubt we'll get together with Janis and a few of the boys at the end of the night. I'll see you both then.'

The couple said goodbye and continued on their walk of discovery. They wandered through the stalls selling everything from mystical books, flowers, music and plenty of other things. Lara decided to get a flower painted in bright colours on each cheek to get into the mood of the festival.

The food stalls were the next port of call. David knew they would have no chance of getting something to eat once the concert began. Two pastrami rolls and two *Cokes* would satisfy their appetites.

The first act, The Association was due to step on stage at 7 pm so they returned to the Kombi to retrieve some things including a few joints and headed for the VIP seats at the front of the stage.

John Phillips from the Mamas and Papas walked on stage at 7.05. He was one of the people who conceived the idea to hold the festival. Papa John welcomed the huge crowd and then introduced The Association.

All six members were dressed in suits and ties – this was not the standard dress during the remainder of the festival. They started their gig with *Enter the Young* followed by *Along Comes Mary* and finished with their hit single *Windy*.

The Association

The crowd was warming up. It was going to be a long night full of music, dancing, and weed.

By the time Eric Burdon and The Animals walked on stage at 9 pm Lara and David had smoked two joints and consumed their pastrami roles. They were mellow.

Eric Burdon - San Franciscan Nights

Chet Helms, Big Brother and Holding Company's manager and the promoter who infused Janis Joplin into the band introduced Eric and the Animals, the only British band to play on Friday night.

Chet Helms Introducing Eric Burdon

Eric Burdon began:

This following program is dedicated to the city and people of San Francisco.
Who may not know it but they are beautiful
And so is their city this is a very personal song
So if the viewer cannot understand it

Particularly those of you who are European residents
Save up all your bread and fly Trans Love Airways to San Francisco USA

Then maybe you'll understand the song, it will be worth it
If not for the sake of this song but for the sake of your own peace of mind.

The song *Warm San Franciscan Night* began.

It was the first time Eric Burden and The Animals performed the song having written it in San Francisco only a few days before.

Following Monterey, it went to number one in Canada and reached number nine in the USA. It also reached number seven in the UK.

The huge crowd loved it as did the other band members standing in the wings including Paul Simon and Art Garfunkel who were the last act to perform for the night.

It was now time for Simon and Garfunkel. John Phillips introduced them as one of the greatest duos of all time.

As the music began the crowd knew it was *Homeward Bound* and many stood and danced to the familiar sound.

The *Sounds of Silence* and the *59th Street Bridge Song (Feelin' Groovy)* were the favourites.

The last song for the day was *Punky's Dilemma*. The throng gradually vacated the arena and grandstands either heading home or to the camping area. Saturday was going to be a huge day.

Saturday, June 17, 1967

Canned Heat

Big Brother & The Holding Company

Al Kooper

Booker T. & The MG's

Country Joe and the Fish

Hugh Masekela

Jefferson Airplane

Laura Nyro

Moby Grape

Otis Redding

Quicksilver Messenger Service

Steve Miller Band

The Byrds

The Electric Flag

The Paul Butterfield Blues Band

Jane and her new boyfriend James, a lawyer who worked with Jane, arrived at Monterey at about 9am having driven from San Francisco. They were expecting to meet up with Lara and David in the VIP area. David had arranged tickets for them.

Jane was particularly looking forward to seeing Big Brother and the Holding Company and Jefferson Airplane. She knew Janis was feeling nervous about appearing, as she had never sung in front of so many rock legends, let alone over 50,000 fans. David and Lara caught sight of their friends as they entered the VIP section.

'Hi you guys, we've been hanging out to see you,' said David.

'We just arrived. How are you two?'

'Great, you missed some great acts last night.'

'Yeah, I know. What were the highlights?'

'It would have to be Eric Burden and The Animals and Simon and Garfunkel. They were magic,' said Lara.

'So, can we sit anywhere or do we have reserved seats?' asked James.

'The seats are reserved. You're apparently sitting next to Lara and me. However, don't get comfortable.'

'Why? What do you mean?'

'Janis and Grace have pulled a few strings. We're going to be in the wings of the stage. We'll not only get a great view we should be able to meet some of the groups.'

'Wow, when do we go?' asked Jane.

'Right now! We were just waiting for you guys to arrive.'

David led the way, passing through two security checkpoints and eventually climbing to the wing of the stage. The other three were in awe – this was a whole new world to them.

Waiting to go on stage was Bob Hite from Canned Heat, the first band up for the afternoon session.

Bob Hite and Elvis Bishop

John Phillips once again made the introductions and Canned Heat played just three songs including *Bullfrog Blues*.

The next group was very familiar to the group of friends. Janis approached them.

'Wish me luck guys. I'm so fuckin' scared I think I'm gonna wet myself.'

The band started their gig with *Down on Me*. That got the crowd's attention. The finale was *Ball 'n' Chain*. It brought the house down, launching Janis Joplin into super stardom.

Janis virtually skipped backstage; she was on cloud nine.

'They loved us. Did you hear that applause?'

'They certainly did Janis. You were brilliant,' said Jane.

'If they could, they'd call you back for more,' said David.

As it turned out, Big Brother and the Holding Company were the only groups that played twice. It wasn't so much by popular demand – the documentary being filmed didn't get footage of their first appearance. Considering the incredible crowd response to their first performance the director insisted they return on Sunday evening. The Sunday night gig was even better received.

Saturday night gave Grace Slick and Jefferson Airplane their opportunity to impress the crowd. Jerry Garcia from Grateful Dead introduced the group.

They began their eight-song gig with *Somebody to Love* and finished with *The Ballad of You and Me* and *Pooneil*.

Jefferson Airplane was one of the groups in which the huge audience was very familiar with; they were regarded as the pioneers of the San Francisco Sound.

134

A little-known singer called Otis Redding performed the last act for the evening.

If Janis was nervous, Otis was petrified. He was used to playing in front of black audiences in the USA and club audiences in Europe, not 50,000 predominantly white hippies from California.

The fact that is was 1 am and drizzling rain didn't help Otis's confidence.

His nerves disappeared when he walked out onto the stage having been introduced by Tommy Smothers, the other half of the Smothers Brothers comedy duo.

Booker T & the MGs started up *Shake* and Otis's performance won the audience over instantly. He then introduced his next song as the one he gave away to some woman. He then sang *Respect* which he had penned two years before. Aretha Franklin recorded it only a month before Monterey.

If the crowd weren't enraptured with Otis by then, they certainly were after he sang the love ballad *I've Been Loving You Too Long.*

Otis had the audience eating out of his hand. He interacted with the 50,000 as though they were in a small nightclub in Paris.

He got them moving again with a cover of *Satisfaction* and then sent them home to bed with *Try a Little Tenderness.*

Otis Redding had been well and truly discovered by mainstream America.

Sunday, June 18

Lara woke at 9 am. David was still sound asleep. They had partied on until 3 am with the likes of Janis, Grace, Brian Jones, Otis Redding, Jimmie Hendrix, Pete Townsend, Mama Cass and John and Michelle Phillips.

She opened the Kombi's door hoping to discover a beautiful morning with bright sunshine and she wasn't disappointed. Jane and James were sitting outside their tent boiling a pot of water for a cup of tea.

'Hi, guys have you got enough water for three?'

'Sure Lars, come and join us. Just bring your mug.'

'So how did you sleep last night?' asked Jane.

'To be honest, I don't remember hitting the pillow.'

'So you and David didn't make love for hours?'

'Not last night we didn't.'

'Yeah, it was a big night. I still can't believe we were in the same space with all those dudes.'

'Well, we've got a huge day ahead.'

'We sure have.'

'It doesn't kick off until after lunch. Have you heard of the Indian guy what his name? Oh, that's right, Ravi Shankar,' said Lara.

'I've heard he's influenced the Beatles quite a bit, having listened to *Sergeant Pepper* I can see how,' said James.

'I better go and wake Dave or he'll sleep all day. See you later on.'

'OK, Lara see you in a little while,' said Jane.

The two couples met up again at 12 noon, strolling around the stalls and eating their lunch at a vegetarian café.

At 1 pm Ravi Shankar and his Indian musicians assembled on stage and the sound of the sitar began to permeate through the concert arena for the next four hours, Ravi Shankar and his accompanying musicians played non-stop.

Rãga Bhimpalasi

Rãga Todi-Rupak Tal (7 Beats)

Tabla Solo In Ektal (12 Beats)

Rãga Shuddha Sarang-Tintal (16 Beats)

Dhun In dadra and fast teental (6 and 16 beats)

Some were mesmerised by the Indian music while others had enough after an hour or so and wandered off to partake of other things.

When Ravi Shankar finally concluded his concert the crowd gave him a standing ovation. Ravi was amazed at the audience reaction. He had never been to a rock festival before and was sceptical that his music would be appreciated at such an event, despite getting assurance from George Harrison and the other Beatles.

18 June Sunday Evening

This was to be the final set a finale to a magnificent festival of music, love and excellent drugs.

Paul Simon walked onto the stage at 7 pm to introduce Blues Project.

Their set was short, just two songs, *Flute Thing* and *Wake Me, Shake Me*.

David had been able to arrange for the group to once again be in the wings for the final night. It was going to be an experience none of them would forget.

Tommy Smothers walked out to introduce Big Brother and the Holding Company for their second performance.

Janis was not so nervous this time she knew what to expect, or she thought she did. She decided to wear a Colin Rose of San Francisco gold outfit and she certainly stood out from any other female artists performing that night.

By the time Janis and the band had completed *Ball and Chain* to finish their six-song set, the crowd was on their feet shouting for more. Big Brother and the Holding Company had been elevated to the status of a major act.

David was working frantically to remove the band's instruments ready for the next act, Buffalo Springfield. Neil Young couldn't play at the festival so a good friend substituted for him. His name was David Crosby.

Jimmie Hendrix was waiting in the Green Room below stage as were the members of The Who and the Mamas and Papas. An argument broke out between Jimmie, and Pete Townsend from the Who about who would play first; neither wanted to follow the other. It became quite heated until John Phillips intervened suggesting he tossed a coin. The coin was tossed Pete called heads and won. The Who was the next act to go on stage.

Buffalo Springfield finished their six-song set with *Pretty Girl Why* and then Eric Burden walked onto the stage to introduce his fellow Englishmen.

'I would like to introduce you to The Who, a group that will destroy you completely in more ways than one.'

The band exploded into *Substitute* followed by *Summertime Blues*.

The British group ripped through *Pictures Of Lily*, *A Quick One, While He's Away*, *Happy Jack*, and *My Generation*. Instead of peace, love and flowers, The Who delivered explosive, energetic rock capped off with Townsend using his electric guitar as a massive axe not only destroying the instrument but some of the other equipment on stage. Keith Moon kicked his drums over and walked off stage, all in all, a great day for the music shops.

Ravi Shankar was standing in the wings next to Lara, Jane and James. He was horrified. He couldn't believe anybody would treat their instruments with so little respect.

Who's Destructive?

Only one band could possibly follow such a performance: The Grateful Dead. Jerry Garcia and the boys simply walked on stage and immediately started up with *Viola Lee Blues* followed by *Cold Rain and Snow*. The final number was *Alligator Caution*. Many commented that it was the purest and best music of the festival; they were the only act that motivated the crowd to get to their feet and dance.

Jerry Garcia on Guitar

Brian Jones founder of the Rolling Stones walked with Jimmie Hendrix up to the stage where Brian introduced the relatively unknown artist.

Brian Jones and Jimmie Hendrix

'I'd like to introduce a very good friend of mine, the best guitarist I've ever heard: Jimmie Hendrix.'

The first howling sounds of Jimmie's Fender Stratocaster were heard throughout the fairground and beyond where thousands were outside the venue listening to the free concert. The 90,000 inside were in awe as Hendrix launched into *Foxy Lady* followed by Like a Rolling Stone, *Rock Me Baby*, *Hey Joe The Wind Cries Mary*. Jimmie had the crowd dumbstruck; they had never heard music like it and when he finished the set with the penultimate song *Purple Haze* they were exhausted. They needed all their energy for the final number *Wild Thing* which went for nearly eight minutes, Jimmie demonstrated all his incredible guitar skills before he sacrificed his Stratocaster by setting it alight and then smashing it on stage. The crowd went berserk, as did his fellow artists watching in the wings including the members of The Who.

Only one showed disgust: Ravi Shankar.

The final act for the festival was the Mamas and Papas.

What a contrast! Jimmie Hendrix's burnt-out Stratocaster had been removed from the stage when Paul Simon introduced the group.

They began their set with '*Straight Shooter* one of their more update numbers. *Spanish Harlem* was next; the two songs that received the loudest applause were *California Dreaming* and *Monday Monday*.

John Phillips then introduced his close friend Scott McKenzie to sing the song he had written for the then unknown artist. John had written it specifically for Monterey.

If You're Going to San Francisco — be sure to wear some flowers in your hair.

The song had been released in early May and by the time he sang it at Monterey it was number four on the charts.

The time had come for the finale of the festival. The Mamas and Papas joined Scott on stage to sing *Dancing in the Streets* with Mama Cass singing the lead vocals. It was a fitting end to what became known as a legendary pop festival.

All the artists performed for free except for one, Ravi Shankar who insisted on being paid $3000.

Proceeds benefited two non-profit organisations: the Monterey County Film Commission and the Monterey International Pop Festival Foundation.

The Monterey International Pop Festival Foundation is a non-profit charitable and educational foundation empowering music-related personal development, creativity, and mental and physical health.

Lara, Jane and the two boys experienced an event that would never be repeated in their lives. They not only had the opportunity to see some of the best performers in the world but they also got to meet and talk with many of them.

The group stayed until Monday afternoon when most of the 90,000 had gone. They returned to San Francisco to continue their lives.

During the time of the festival over 100 allied soldiers were killed in Vietnam.

Lara and David were driving through Carmel when they decided to stop at a spot overlooking the ocean and make a cup of coffee.

'I'm still feeling euphoric Dave. That was a great three days. Janis's singing was amazing – she's going to conquer the world.'

'I hope so, depending on whether she stays around that long.'

'What do you mean?'

'She's back on the drugs.'

'Oh no, she's not using speed again is she?'

'I'm afraid it's heavier than that. She's shooting up heroin.'

'How do you know?'

'I caught her with a needle in her arm at Monterey just before she went on the second time.'

'You're her friend. Did you try and stop her?'

'She told me to mind my own business and fuck off.'

'That's sad.'

David and Lara continued their trip back to San Francisco in near silence, both deep in thought.

GOOD MORNING VIETNAM

CHAPTER 21

Life got back to normal for Lara and David once they returned from Monterey, and the couple were enjoying living in the beautiful house in Lower Haight. They had plenty of visitors including Jane and James, plus Pearl and Grace and a few of the musicians they met at the festival.

Lara had also made friends with a few of her fellow interns from John Hopkins. They too were regular visitors.

Lara resumed her internship at John Hopkins Hospital while David continued his duties as a roadie for Big Brother and the Holding Company. As the band became more and more popular, he was required to travel across America extensively. Lara didn't mind the time alone, but always welcomed him home enthusiastically.

1968

Martin Luther King assassinated

President John Kennedy assassinated

Tet Offensive Vietnam

24th March 1968

Dr De Neville had had a mixed day at the John Hopkins. She assisted Dr Edwards in an emergency delivery of a baby whose mother had been in a car accident. The baby survived, its mother and father didn't. Lara could relate to what this child would encounter over the coming years.

Working in the emergency department gave Lara a taste of pretty much every conceivable injury and its treatment, including some wild and wonderful cases, which were usually discussed over a drink with David and friends.

One example was where a neighbour of a newlywed couple was worried when she didn't hear her rather noisy neighbours for a while. A few days later, she peered through their letterbox and the windows. But there was no sign of anyone. Concerned for the young couple, she called the police. The officers promptly broke down the door and searched the house. They found the young woman gagged and tied to the bed naked. Her husband was lying on the floor with two broken legs, wearing a Superman outfit. They later explained that they had been engaged in a superhero role-playing fantasy, and the costumed husband had broken his legs attempting to jump onto his wife from atop the dresser. Of course, the woman was unable to help him!

Both were brought into the emergency ward. She was suffering from dehydration and he was still in his Superman outfit.

Another case, which caused lots of laughter amongst their friends, was where an unconscious thirty-year-old man was brought into Emergency. His girlfriend had found him lying naked on the floor of his bathroom and called an ambulance. He was found to have a large lump on the top of his head and strangely, several scratches on his scrotum. Lara decided the lump was possibly caused by a fall or a knock to the head. However, the source of the scratches remained a mystery until he woke up and provided Lara with the following explanation. He said he had been cleaning his bathtub while naked having just stepped out of the shower. He had been kneeling on the floor beside the tub when his cat, apparently transfixed by the rhythmic swaying of his scrotum, lunged forward, sinking its claws into this pendulous target. This caused the man to rocket upward, striking his head on the top frame of the shower door.

Lara arrived home at about 7 pm looking forward to sharing a bottle of wine with David. She found him in the back room drinking a whisky.

'Hi, babe. You've started without me – how come?'

David looked at her with glazed eyes. It was obviously not his first drink for the day.

'I received this today.'

He passed a typed letter over to his girlfriend. She read it and gasped.

'Yeah, that was my reaction too. I can't believe it.'

The letter was from the US Defence Department informing him he'd been drafted into the Army for two years.

'Why you?'

'Think about it, babe. I'm a twenty-four-year-old university drop-out from a small town in Texas. I'm a perfect candidate.'

'But you intend to re-enrol next year. Don't they take that into account?'

'Not at all, as far as they're concerned I'm a drop-out who needs a bloody good haircut.'

'How did they find you?'

'My parents forwarded the letter on.'

'You could plead that you're a conscientious objector.'

'Yeah, right. I'd end up in some stinking prison for two or three years. I'd rather go to Vietnam.'

'So, when do you have to report to the army?'

'The letter states May 1st.'

'That's only five weeks away.'

'Yeah, I know it doesn't give us much time does it?'

'Fuck it; I didn't see this coming, babe. Why don't you pour me a drink then let's go out for dinner,' said Lara.

Over dinner at the Café Trieste, the two lovers discussed their immediate plans. David had to make his way back to Port Arthur Texas to see his folks then report in at Fort Sam in Houston about an hour and a half away from his hometown.

'So how were you thinking of getting back to Texas?'

'I don't know, I suppose I'll catch a Greyhound bus or two or three.'

'I've got an idea. I can get about two weeks leave from the hospital so why don't I come with you, and we can drive the Kombi to Texas.'

'That means you've got to drive back alone,'

'I'm a big girl. I don't have a problem with that. Just think, babe. It gives us more time together and I get to meet your parents.'

'I'm not sure you want to do that.'

'Of course I do, you've always spoken fondly of them. They can't be all that bad. Right, that's settled. Now let's go home. We've only got about 35 more opportunities to make love before you leave.'

'I'm with you, honey.'

They decided to depart San Francisco on 15 April taking eight days to make the journey, stopping at trailer parks along the way.

Lara had arranged a surprise going-away party for David on the 13th. She invited the band members from Big Brother and the Holding Company, Jefferson Airplane, Grateful Dead and the Mommas and the Papas plus their roadies and various other friends: about fifty people in all.

David walked into the house and got the surprise of his life. Although he was shocked he was delighted at the chance to say farewell to his friends. It was a great night with all sorts of alcohol and drugs being consumed. It was past 3 am before they got to bed.

April 15

Lara and David set off on their long journey at 5 am heading for Los Angeles. The coast road was fantastic. Although they had driven a short section of this road before when attending the Monterey Pop Festival, the remaining 350-mile stretch promised magnificent beaches, towering mountains, and uninterrupted views of the Pacific Ocean.

The first town encountered on the journey was Santa Cruz where they pulled into the parking lot overlooking the amusement park and admired the beach. Their intention was to continue and have lunch at Carmel by the Sea.

The drive to Carmel only took the Kombi an hour and they were both entranced with the beautiful village. This is where Lara and David decided to camp for the first night.

Carmel Village

The following morning they approached the stretch of coastline called the Big Sur. It was breathtaking. Big Sur is a rugged stretch of California's central coast between Carmel and San Simeon, bordered to the east by the Santa Lucia Mountains and the west by the Pacific Ocean.

Approaching Big Sur

They drove on to Santa Barbara where they camped for the night. The next day they would drive into Los Angeles and head for Phoenix Arizona, where the two travellers had planned to stay.

All in all Lara and David spent eight days on the road staying at Tucson, Las Cruses and San Antonio. On the eighth day they arrived in Houston, and David found a telephone booth to ring his parents to let them know their arrival was imminent.

The draftee drove the Kombi into the driveway of his boyhood home and beeped the horn three times. Both his parents came out the front entrance waving and smiling.

The next few days were enjoyable. Lara got on with both parents, Jim and Felicity, very well and David seemed relaxed despite what lay ahead.

'Dave, why don't you show me where Janis lived?'

'It's not much to look at, Lars. The house is similar to this house.'

'Well, I'd still like to see it. I can tell her I saw it when I get back to San Francisco.'

'OK, let's go. We can walk from here.'

Janis Joplin's Girlhood Home

The family and Lara had a BBQ for their final meal before David was to be transported to Fort Sam and his new life. On the same day Lara would begin her long journey home.

It was a great evening with plenty of beer and wine consumed. Lara suggested to David they walk down to the beach located only half a mile from the house. They sat on the sand watching the small waves breaking on the shoreline.

'David, I want to tell you more about myself before you go.'

'Oh no! You're a mother of three who murdered her husband for the life insurance.'

'Don't be stupid. However, there are things you should know about me.'

'OK babe. What do I need to know?'

'I've already told you that both my parents were killed in a boating accident on the Chesapeake Bay when I was six.'

'Yes.'

'And you know I was raised by my nanny. What I haven't told you is my father was an Earl, and my mother was a Countess.'

'Does that mean you're a Countess?'

'It does, not that I use the title.'

'Wow, so I've been going out with royalty.'

'Hardly. I'm not the Queen of England.'

'Anything else I should know?'

'Well, yes there is. I told you I inherited some money from my parents' estate. That's how I purchased the house and the Kombi. Well, in fact, I inherited quite a bit of money.'

'Really? How much?'

'In US Dollars about $100,000,000.'

'Holy shit.'

'Yes, I know what you mean. It's always been a concern of mine that I could meet someone who loved me for who I am and not how rich I am.

'You David are that man; I love you, and I know you love me. When you serve your time in the Army, I want us to continue our relationship.'

'You're right, Lara. I do love you. I just have to get my head around what you've just told me.'

'I want to spend the rest of my life with you, David. Hopefully you feel the same.'

'I do babe, I really do.'

They walked back to the house hand in hand in reflective silence.

The next morning the five people at the breakfast table were pensive. They all knew the possibility of David not returning from Vietnam was real.

Jim went out to the garage to start up his pride and joy, his three-month-old Chevy Impala.

The Benson family began the drive to Fort Sam at 9 am arriving at 10.30. There were many people from Fort Arthur of which the Bensons knew many, all saying goodbye to their sons. Lara felt like a fish out of water but she also felt sombre she knew she wouldn't see her man for a long time.

David did feel some consolation knowing that many of his school pals were also being conscripted on the same day.

The time came when all the draftees were required to go through the fort's gates and into the unknown. Last minute kisses and handshakes were given to the young men. Lara had trouble letting go of David, but finally, she looked him in the eye and whispered, 'I love you, come back to me.'

David

David and the other draftees walked through the gates. Two marines holding M3 sub-machine guns were standing either side.

They were instructed to enter a large hall and fall into line. There they were all given a short physical examination. The next step was an interview where each draftee was asked a series of questions to determine if they were mentally fit and if they were homosexuals or communists. Some were rejected, including an old school friend of David's. He was surprised – he knew Gary wasn't a homosexual or communist with a mental problem.

The next step was to enter another hall where there were lines painted on the floor with an enormous American flag on the front wall.

They were instructed to line up along the lines and then step forward to be 'voluntarily' sworn in. By stepping forward, David had just become a 'registrant' soldier. You're in the Army now son.

The oath of allegiance was administered.

'I David Benson do solemnly swear that I will bear true faith and allegiance to the Constitution of the United States of America and will defend it against all enemies foreign and domestic, and will obey the orders of the President and the officers appointed over me, so help me God.'

David now realised he was the property of the United States Army.

The men were organised into smaller groups. Once that was achieved a huge, ugly, and very mean sergeant began yelling at David's group to get into formation and march to their barrack hut. They placed their bags on the bunks, and then they were ordered to the barber's hut where they were shorn. David was not keen about the cut but had no choice.

The next eight weeks was hard going marching, running, push-ups and more push-ups. By the end of the basic training David and his army pals were a lot fitter than they had ever been.

The Army decided that since David had completed three years of a medical degree he should undergo another eight weeks of specialist medical unit training. At the end of the course, he would be classified as an assistant army medic. He was now Private First-class, just one up from a grunt.

He was informed that he was being deployed to Vietnam and was given 30 days leave before his departure. He returned home to Port Arthur for a few days with his parents and then flew to San Francisco via Los Angeles to spend the remainder of his time with Lara.

All his old friends from San Francisco were suitably impressed with his new hairstyle, giving him a hard time. David was especially pleased to see Jane and James. He did encounter some unpleasant moments around Haight-Ashbury where some hippies spat on him and called him a murderer. The anti-war movement at that time was vicious.

Overall Lara and he had a great time attending concerts, eating out, drinking good wine and making love.

David had come to terms with Lara's title and wealth; she was still the same girl he had fallen in love with at the concert.

When his leave had expired, he was due to report to Oakland Army Terminal to begin his processing for deployment to Vietnam.

Saying goodbye to Lara was tough. They both knew the dangers which confronted him. They ate at their favourite restaurant, Café Trieste, returning home to make love for what could be the last for a very long time.

Next morning Lara drove David to Oakland. Their farewell was no easier the second time.

Two days later PFC David Benson boarded a Tiger Airlines plane bound for Vietnam 25 hours flying time away.

David wrote a letter to Lara once he had settled into his barracks at Bien Hoa.

August 10, 1968

Dear Lara,

I thought I would drop you a line just to let you know what's been happening.

The plane stopped in Hawaii for fuel and a change of aircrew; we were holed up in an abandoned hanger while this took place. We're - boarded the plane and a roll call was taken; one guy was missing probably on his way to Waikiki. We then flew to Midway Island and took on fuel and headed for Guam where we took on more fuel and changed flight crews.

Nobody spoke much on the final leg we all knew things were only going to get worse, I did manage a few catnaps, but I was mainly thinking about you, darling.

An announcement was made by the flight attendant 'Fasten your seatbelts and prepare for landing.'

I looked out the window at the vast darkness only a small point of light now and then indicated human habitation.

We began to descend, and soon the plane was taxiing along the Bien Hoa Airbase runway, which is about 20 miles from Saigon.

The time was 11.30 pm we were preparing to disembark when an announcement came over the speaker thanking us all for Flying Tiger Airlines, and hoping we would be flying back home with Tiger in twelve months time.

We all agreed that would be our preference.'

Bien Hoa Airbase

When the crew opened the plane doors we disembarked via mobile stairs, as soon as we hit the tarmac a wall of oppressive sticky heat greeted us. The sweat began running down our faces, and the shirts on our backs became drenched. I had been to many airports around the world before but nothing like this one, the sounds of choppers landing and taking off, jets roaring down the runway and trucks and jeeps going which way and that.

We were walking toward a building looking at the activity around us when suddenly a huge explosion occurred and then another. The sergeant escorting us yelled. 'Get inside quick double time. We didn't need any persuasion we rushed inside the closest building. I can tell you Lara I was shit scared. Everybody else in the building was just going about their business as though nothing had happened. An officer in green jungle fatigues yelled out 'OK it's over now just calm down.' He explained that the airport had been under attack by Viet Kong rockets, which apparently were a regular occurrence. 'Don't worry fellas you'll get used to it.'

'I don't think so.'

I find out tomorrow which hospital I'll be posted to.

I miss you already Lars.

Love

David

xxxx

HAMBURGER HILL

DO YOU WANT FRIES WITH THAT?

CHAPTER 22

Private David Benson was assigned to the 85th Evacuation Hospital at Phu Bai. He had been at the hospital only one day when a call went out for several air ambulances to be deployed. He boarded the helicopter along with several Marines. It was the regular practice to have two escort helicopters protecting each air ambulance.

Mobile Army Surgical Hospital (MASH)

They would be flying into an area which was known to be controlled by the Viet Kong. Apparently, an armoured patrol had been ambushed. Although the US troops had been able to repel the attack, many had been wounded or killed. David and his team were assigned the task of taking the wounded back to the MASH at Phu Bai airbase.

Under Attack

The chopper circled the battlefield several times ensuring the area was secure. They then landed and began retrieving the wounded soldiers.

The helicopter took off heading back to Phu Bai; expectations for saving these soldiers were high. This experience blooded David for what to expect over the coming twelve months.

He finished up for the day and made his way to the amenities block and showered.

Meals were taken in a large shed, rows and rows of tables and bench seats. David walked in, not knowing where he should sit. He heard his name being called – it was one of the crew from the day's operation.

David sat down next to the medic. They hadn't introduced themselves in the chopper.

'Hi, my name is Steven.'

'Hi, I'm David.'

'Yeah, I know.'

'Seeing we'll be working together I thought we should find out a little about each other.'

'Sounds reasonable.'

The two men lined up to get their evening meal of hamburgers, chips and salad.

'Geez, my dad fought in the Second World War. He complained that the food was terrible. This looks OK,' said Steven.

'Sure does, better than SPAM.'

'Where are you from, Dave?'

'Originally Texas, a small town near Houston called Port Arthur.'

'Port Arthur? Isn't that where Janis Joplin came from?'

'How'd you know that?'

'I'm one of her greatest fans.'

'Really. Yeah she lived down the street from me.'

'Did you know her?'

'I did, very well.'

David went onto to explain his role as a roadie and the groups he got to know in San Francisco.

'Fucking hell, you're almost a celebrity.'

'I don't think so, Steven. I lugged famous people's gear around.'

'Well, I don't care what you say. You're the first person I've met who knows Janis Joplin, Jerry Garcia, Grace Slick and whole bunch of other celebrities.'

'Well I don't know about you Steven, but I'm exhausted. I think I'll make my way to my tent and try and rest up a bit.'

'Ok Dave, you don't mind if I call you that do you?'

'Not all Steve.'

'Goodnight.'

'Goodnight.'

David and Steve performed several rescue missions over the next few months. There were some scary moments with their helicopter being hit by enemy fire, but no major incidents. That was until the Battle of Hamburger Hill.

In 1969, US troops began Operation Apache Snow with the goal of clearing the People's Army of Vietnam from the A Shau Valley in South Vietnam. Located near the border with Laos, the valley had become an infiltration route into South Vietnam and a haven for PAVN forces.

The battle took place on a hill known as Hill 937 on United States Army maps.

However, the United States troops who attacked the hill named it Hamburger Hill in reference to a similar battle during the Korean War which was known as The Battle of Pork Chop Hill. However, both of these battles were pointless attacks on locations that had little strategic importance to the outcome of the war and resulted in heavy losses to the US and South Vietnamese forces.

The People's Army of North Vietnam, some 800 regular troops, were well entrenched in an elevated position. The United States and South Vietnamese troops numbered some 1800 personnel.

The battle was uncharacteristic of the fighting in the Vietnam War, since it involved large troop units on both sides and because the enemy did not use the ploy of manoeuvre, but instead chose to defend their positions on Dong Ap Bia. The result was a very bloody battle with high casualties sustained by all units, thus prompting American troops to call the objective 'Hamburger Hill.'

While the enemy's tactics were out of the ordinary, the United States routinely emphasised firepower, including heavy artillery, napalm, and B-52 'Arc Light' air strikes. Nonetheless, the enemy's defensive skills against this tactic, together with his persistence, meant that eventually, his positions had to be assaulted by infantry, and the result was ferocious combat, often hand to hand. After eleven days, the enemy retreated to sanctuaries in Laos. One week later, Hamburger Hill was abandoned by the triumphant American troops. This was a normal consequence of battles in Vietnam, particularly in areas like the A Shau Valley, which were remote and lightly populated. The basic strategy of both sides was attrition, not the occupation of captured territory.

The battle of Hamburger Hill was comparable to other engagements during the war. Enemy losses were much higher than American and South Vietnamese casualties, the enemy resolved the battle by retreating without pursuit by American forces, and the battlefield was abandoned shortly after the end of hostilities.

David and Steve had made several runs picking up wounded soldiers. Many of the injuries were horrific and the hospital at the base was having real difficulty keeping up with the volume.

They had just picked up several wounded when David spotted a soldier standing next to a dead soldier with two wounded behind him.

He yelled to the pilot asking whether they could land and pick up the wounded. The pilot agreed, knowing it was a major risk.

The helicopter landed as close to the casualties as possible. Dave and Steve jumped out with a stretcher in hand and ferried the two wounded Americans back to the chopper. They yelled out to the pilot to take off and the pilot lifted his aircraft and banked steeply; bullets and shells were filling the air. They reached an altitude where they thought they were out of harm's way when a massive explosion rocked the aircraft. The pilot tried to control the descent, but with the rotor severely damaged the chopper was unmanageable. The air ambulance came crashing down, landing in a shallow ravine. The pilot screamed out for everybody to abandon the helicopter in case it exploded.

Steve looked over at David. He was horrified: his pal's head had been almost blown off by a large piece of shrapnel. As it happened, Dave was the only casualty.

Chopper Down

Steve sat on the bank, his head in his hands trying to comprehend what had just happened. One minute he was helping David bandage a severely wounded soldier, the next minute his good friend was dead. Another chopper landed to transfer the survivors back to base, where ironically all the wounded recovered. David was the only casualty.

Lara had finished her shift in the John Hopkins Casualty Ward. It had been a long night with several gunshot wounds and two major motor vehicle accidents with serious injuries to treat. She drove home in her beloved Kombi, and as she drove Lara was thinking about the letter she'd received from the Royal Free London Hospital, the most prestigious plastic surgery hospital in Britain. She'd been accepted to study and practise in the Reconstructive Plastic Surgery Department. Her only concern was leaving America and David. She hoped he would agree to come with her and finish his degree at Oxford. David was due to call her that night so she would discuss it with him then. The military had organised what they called MARS (Military Affiliate Radio Service) to be deployed throughout Vietnam. This allowed for soldiers and sailors to be able to communicate with loved ones back home, albeit for five minutes.

Lara arrived home, showered and dressed in a comfortable kaftan she poured herself a glass of wine and waited for his call.

At 8 pm the telephone rang; she picked up the receiver.

'Hello darling, how are you?'

'Lara, it's not David. It's Jim, David's father.'

'Oh, hello Jim. This is a pleasant surprise.'

'Lara, I have some tragic news.'

'No, don't tell me. I don't want to hear.'

'I'm so sorry Lara. Felicity and I are also devastated.'

'When?'

'Two days ago.'

Lara began crying uncontrollably. She couldn't comprehend that she would never see David, her one true love, ever again.

'Jim. I can't speak right now ...'

'I know Lara, I know. We'll speak again soon.'

The grief-stricken woman could not stop crying. She yelled and screamed at everybody and anything. She blamed the US Army, the Government and herself for allowing the man she loved to be taken from her. Eventually exhausted, she went to bed. She could smell David's scent on the bedclothes. She finally sobbed herself to sleep constantly waking throughout the night.

Lara rang the hospital next morning explaining why she wouldn't be in for a few days. She rang Jane and told her the news. Jane was horrified and promised to come around that morning; she had no cases that day.

When Jane arrived the two friends hugged each other and cried into each other's shoulders for what seemed an hour.

'Babe, have you got any whisky? That's what we both need right now.'

'Yes, David always keeps a bottle.'

The two friends just looked at each other and begun hugging and crying again.

'Where's the bottle, Lars?'

'In the kitchen on the top shelf.'

'I've got it, *Macallans* 18 year-old. It deserves the top shelf.'

Jane poured two generous glasses and the two distraught women moved out to the garden room.

'So Lars, I know it's early days, but have you given any thought about what you might do?'

'I received a letter yesterday informing me I've been accepted to do post-graduate work at Royal Free London Hospital.'

'Is that good?'

'It sure is. They're the best plastic surgery teaching hospital in Britain.'

'So I take it you're going to accept?'

'Yes, I'd already decided to take it before I learnt about David.'

'When do you take up the post?'

'Next January.'

'Are you going back to England soon?'

'Well with what's just happened ... I think I will.'

'You'll have no trouble selling this beautiful house.'

'Oh, I wouldn't sell it. I'll rent it out for a while just to see what happens.'

'Well, if you want a good tenant I know David Crosby is looking around for a place to rent.'

'I'd be happy to rent it to him.'

'OK, I'll tell him to contact you in a couple of weeks.'

'Fine.'

Lara rang Jim and Felicity the following day to discover when David would be arriving home. She was notified the casket was due in Port Arthur the next Friday, three days away. The funeral had been organised for the following Wednesday.

'Jim, I would like to attend the funeral.'

'Of course, Lara we thought you would attend. How are you coping?'

'Reasonable, not great. How about you two?'

'I'm OK. Felicity is finding it very difficult.'

'Yes, I can understand that.'

'Felicity and I would like you to stay with us.'

'That's very kind of you Jim, thank you. I'll call you back when I book my air tickets.'

'OK, Lara we'll pick you up from Houston.'

'That would be very kind of you.''Not at all. See you soon.'

Lara had just hung up the telephone when it rang.

'Hello, this is Lara.'

'Lara it's Janis. I've just heard about David, you poor baby.'

'Thanks for calling Janis. Yes, I'm in total shock.'

'Can I come around and see you?'

'If you like. When?'

'Now. I can be there in five minutes.'

'OK, I'll put the kettle on.'

'Fuck the kettle I'll bring a bottle of *Southern Comfort*.'

'See you soon.'

True to her word Janis arrived within five minutes with the familiar bottle of whisky.

'Hi Janis, come on in.'

'I'm so sorry Lara. I know how close you and David were. Can I give you a hug?'

The two women hugged, both with tears streaming down their faces.

'Right, let's have a drink. I think we both need one. Where do you keep your whisky glasses?'

'I'll get them, they're in the kitchen hutch.'

Janis took on the pouring duties, ensuring they were triples.

'Where will we sit, babe?'

'Out in the garden room, it's less formal. And it's where David and I would sit when we had our pre-dinner drink.'

The two friends made a toast to David, which made both of them cry again.

'I feel guilty Lara. It was me who suggested to him that he have a two-year sabbatical from med school and become a roadie for the band. If he'd continued, he wouldn't have been drafted.'

'You can't blame yourself, Janis. Ultimately it was David's decision.'

'Yeah, I suppose you're right. Do you know when the funeral is?'

'This coming Wednesday. Do you intend to go?'

'No, I've thought about it but if I attend the media will make it into a circus. That's not what David's parents or you would want. It's sad, but that's the reality of the situation.'

'You're right, it is sad.'

'I have had an idea though. But it requires your approval.'

'What?'

'I'd like to arrange a memorial concert for David in a few weeks time, when things have settled down a bit. David wasn't just a roadie. He was a much-loved person by not only the members of the band but other bands as well.'

'Janis that sounds fantastic! David would love it.'

'OK, leave it with me. I'll keep you posted as we get things organised.'

Janis left the house, excited that her idea for a memorial concert would come to fruition.

When Janis arrived back at her Haight-Ashbury home she began calling her musician friends including the members of her new backing group the Kozmic Blues Band. The first person she called was Sam Andrew. He'd been the lead guitarist with Janis's first group, Big Brother and the Holding Company, and was like a brother to the singer. Sam had followed Janis over to the new band.

The next person she called was Mama Cass who was very close to David. Mama Cass agreed to consult the other members of the singing group and was confident they'd agree. Janis also called Grace Slick, who decided immediately on behalf of her band, Jefferson Airplane.

Janis was pleased with her efforts. The next task was to find a suitable venue. Her preference was Fillmore West so she called Bill Graham the owner who agreed depending on an appropriate date. After discussion with the bands and Bill, it was decided that the date for the Concert for David would be June 30.

The arrangements for David's funeral had been finalised: it would be held on 1 June at the Church of Christ in Port Arthur.

His casket was now on US soil having been flown home by a transport plane.

1 June Port Arthur Texas

Lara had flown to Houston from San Francisco on May 30 and Jim picked her up and drove her back to Port Arthur.

The drive back was a solemn affair. Except for some idle conversation they didn't discuss David's tragic death.

Felicity met them at the front door and gave Lara a long hug. They ate dinner together and retired early; the next day would be sad and exhausting.

The funeral was scheduled for 10 am. Tithe Bensons had no idea how many mourners would attend and they were surprised that the church overflowed to the outside lawn. It was estimated that over two hundred people were at the service.

The funeral was traditional with several hymns and a moving sermon by the minister, with the eulogy delivered by one of David's school friends, Gary Carson. The only digression from the traditional service was a beautiful rendition of *Blue Moon* sung by Lisbeth Jackson, another school friend. Apparently it was David's favourite song.

The wake was held at the Bensons' house with fifty people showing their respect.

Lara flew home the next day after what had been a moving but draining experience. On the plane she reflected on her life. Thus far, she had lost her parents when she was six years old, her best friend Megan at eight, her cousin Andrew, and now the only true love of her life, David. All the people she had loved had been taken away from her.

She drove home from the airport having parked in the long-term car park. Entering the house, she was overwhelmed by an intense feeling of loneliness.

Farewell My Love

CHAPTER 23

Lara called Janis to see how the memorial concert was coming together.

'Hi, Pearl, it's Lara. I'm back from beautiful downtown Port Arthur.'

'Hi, babe. How'd it all go?'

'Funerals are never pleasant. Especially saying goodbye to the one you love more than life itself. However, as far as funerals go it was good.'

'How many came along?'

'Jim told me it was close to 200.'

'Wow, that's amazing. I suppose I wouldn't know most of them.'

'The highlight was a friend of David's Lisbeth Jackson. She sang *Blue Moon.*'

'I know the song and her, but I wonder why she chose that?

'Apparently it was one of David's favourites from when he was a boy.'

'I didn't know that.'

'So how's the memorial concert coming along?'

'Great! We've got my new band, naturally. Plus the Mamas and Papas and Jefferson Airplane. There may be some last minute acts to throw their hats in the ring, but no promises.'

'Have you got a venue?'

'Yeah, Fillmore West.'

'Cool, what date?'

'June 30. It's a Sunday night.'

'It all sounds great, Janis. Thank you so much.'

'Don't thank me, it's the least I could do.'

'I'll see you soon, no doubt?'

'How about I call in tomorrow?'

'Yes, that's fine. I don't start back at the hospital until Monday.'

Janis called in for a coffee the following morning to discuss some of the finer points of the concert.

'Lara, I've been thinking about *Blue Moon*, seeing it was David's favourite, why don't we sing it at the concert?'

'Yeah, that would be great.'

'Not me, it doesn't suit my voice, but the Mama and Papas would be perfect.'

'Do you think they'd do it?'

'I don't know, but it doesn't hurt to ask does it?'

Janis got into her psychedelic Porsche and zoomed off.

Lara resumed her work in the casualty ward at John Hopkins, just the usual: stab wounds, car accidents, strokes, etc.

She contacted Royal Free London Hospital accepting the position. This left her with three months living in San Francisco.

The day of David's concert arrived. It was advertised as a charity event whereby admission fees would be donated to various not-for-profit organisations.

The seating capacity was 1200 and all seats had been sold well before the concert. The host for the evening was John Phillips from the Mamas and Papas.

At 8 pm John walked out on stage and welcomed the audience to what he called a very special evening. He described David as a wonderful human being.

The set list for the concert was as follows:

Janis Joplin and the Kozmic Blues Band

Piece of My Heart

Farewell Song (to David)

Bye Bye Baby

Jefferson Airplane with Grace Slick

My Best Friend

Volunteers

Somebody to Love

Grateful Dead

Viola Lee Blues

The Golden Road

Dark Star

Mamas and Papas

Dream a Little Dream of Me

California Dreaming

Dedicated to the One I Love

Blue Moon

As the Mamas and Papas completed *Dedicated to the One I Love* to rapturous applause, Janis Joplin, Grace Slick and a last minute inclusion, Jimmie Hendrix, joined the group.

Jimmie began the gentle haunting riff of *Blue Moon*, and the friends of David Benson sang his favourite tune like it had never been sung before.

Blue Moon Lyrics

I only want to say

That if there is a way

I want my baby back with me

'Cause he's my true love, my only one, don't you see?

And on that fateful day

Perhaps in the new sun of May

My baby walks back into my arms

I'll keep him beside me forever from harm

You see I was afraid

to let my baby stray

I kept him too tightly by my side

And then one sad day, he went away and he died

Blue moon, you saw me standing alone

without a dream in my heart

without a love of my own

Blue moon, you knew just what I was there for

you heard me saying a prayer for

someone I really could care for

169

I only want to say

that, if there is a way

I want my baby back with me

'Cause he's my true love, my only one, don't you see?

Good Bye David.

Two months later the biggest single music event in world history took place at Woodstock in New York State. Many of the performers were David's friends. He would have loved it.

BEND ME SHAPE ME

CHAPTER 24

1969

ARPANET, the Precursor of the Internet, created

Manson Family Murders

Neil Armstrong becomes the first man to walk on the moon

1 August 1969

Lara completed her last day at John Hopkins Hospital. She had enjoyed her two years there learning emergency medicine at its highest level.

The medical staff chipped in to buy a Black Forest cake, which didn't quite go around. The Chief Physician gave a speech acknowledging Lara as a fine doctor and a team player.

After saying goodbye to her colleagues, she returned to her empty, lonely home. Or so she thought – a group of her closest friends including Jane, Janis, and Grace were waiting for her on the footpath.

'What are you all doing here?'

'You didn't think we'd let you fly off to England without a goodbye drink did you?' said Jane.

'That's kind of you. But I don't think I have any grog left in the house.'

'We brought our own. Now come on, open up. We feel a bit exposed out here,' said David Crosby.

Lara opened the front door and her friends piled in. Before she knew it, there were champagne corks popping and *Southern Comfort* being consumed.

More friends arrived over the next hour and by the end of the night more than thirty people had passed through the front door. When the last guests departed, she looked around at the mess that needed to be cleaned up prior to her departure early next morning.

Thankfully David Crosby had promised to clean it up before moving in. Lara climbed the stairs to her bedroom, undressed and flopped into bed. It had been a very long day. She set the alarm for 5 am. That would give her plenty of time to get to the airport. Sam Andrew from Janis's band had purchased the Kombi and she knew it would be much loved.

Lara caught a cab to the airport and boarded the Pan Am 747 settling into the Business Class seat. The flight would take ten and a half hours and she was hopeful of sleeping a good part of the way.

It had been fortunate that the tenants in the South Kensington townhouse had not renewed their lease, allowing Lara to move in straight away.

Lisbeth had arranged for it to be cleaned and appropriate furniture to be purchased before Lara's arrival.

Lara arrived at the townhouse having caught a taxi from Heathrow. It was 10 am and she was exhausted and hungry. Lisbeth greeted her at the front door. It had been two years since they last saw each other. Lisbeth hugged the weary traveller and helped with her luggage. Brunch had been placed in the back garden with fresh fruit and pastries, juice and hot coffee.

Once brunch had been consumed, Lara brought Lisbeth up-to-date with what had been happening in her life while in America. Although they had spoken on the telephone regularly, face to face was always so much better.

Lara was due to begin her role as assistant surgeon to Dr Graham Sutton, who was widely regarded as the best reconstructive plastic surgeon in Britain, if not the world. Her employment would begin in January 1970.

Her life in San Francisco had been fantastic, with plenty of friends, David and some amazing music that kept her happy.

In London, she knew no-one, which she wasn't overly concerned about. She'd been hurt too many times, losing all the people she'd loved.

1970

The Beatles break up.

PLO hijacks five planes.

National Guard shoots and kills four student protesters.

4 January 1970

Lara was nervous. She was about to begin the most important day in her career under the tutelage of the most revered surgeon on the planet.

Dr Graham Sutton was not only known for his brilliance, he had a reputation as a ladies' man. Lara was now 28 with long blonde hair, and an angelic face and her figure could have allowed her to be a model.

Dr Lara de Neville

She knew she would have to keep him at arms' length, despite working with him so closely.

She approached the front desk introducing herself and asking for Dr Sutton. The receptionist attempted to call him in his office but didn't get a reply. She checked the medical schedule and discovered he was operating on an emergency case that had been admitted early that morning. Lara was told to register at personnel and read a copy of the hospital's operations manual until Dr Sutton became available.

Lara was given instructions by the personnel officer as to where Dr Sutton's offices were located. She eventually found them and settled in to read the manual.

At about noon, Dr Sutton arrived back from the operating theatre. He walked straight past Lara, ignoring her completely. It wasn't until his receptionist informed him that the new doctor was waiting for him that he re-entered reception.

'So you're Dr de Neville? I'm sorry I thought you must have been a patient.'

'Well, that's a compliment.'

'Sorry, you know what I mean.'

'I think I do.'

'Come into my office and we can have a chat.'

The two doctors entered Dr Sutton's large tastefully decorated office. It had a view over the hospital's gardens and had several modern artworks that Lara estimated would be worth a small fortune.

'Take a seat, Lara. Can I get Margaret to get you a coffee? I know I'm due for one after this morning's surgery.'

'Yes, that would be nice. Thank you, doctor.'

'Let's start off on the right track: I'm Graham.'

'OK, Graham.'

Graham asked his secretary to organise two strong coffees and some biscuits.

'How did you enjoy your time at John Hopkins, Lara?'

'I loved it. Especially the bullet and stab wounds. No seriously, it's an excellent teaching hospital. I learnt a lot.'

'So why come back to England?'

'I've always believed this hospital would be where I could best learn reconstructive plastic surgery.'

'Why reconstructive and not tits and bums?'

'You have a way with words, Graham! The fact is that both my parents were reconstructive plastic surgeons. Although I didn't know them well, I always admired their profession and their reputations.'

'Yes, I must admit I know of your parents and their work, particularly regarding soldiers wounds.'

'Really?'

'I understand they died when you were quite young?'

'Yes, I was only six.'

'That's sad. Well, getting on with business, we have a busy week ahead: two part facial reconstructions resulting from car accidents and a burns patient.'

'I'm looking forward to it.'

'Have you registered with personnel yet and been given the dreaded operations manual to read?'

'Yes to both questions.'

'OK, well let's have lunch, and you can follow me on my afternoon round.'

'OK.'

Lara enjoyed working with Graham. He gradually let her take more and more responsibility in the operating theatre. At the end of her first year, she had performed several operations as the lead surgeon.

On weekends, she would return to Westmoreland where Lisbeth still managed the estate. She was now 49, twenty years older than Lara. It seemed strange to them both that as a young girl Lisbeth was her nanny and then her legal guardian. Now they were the closest of friends.

The weekends were taken up mainly by two activities, horse riding and golf.

Both Lara and Lisbeth had joined Oak Manor Golf Club in Taunton not far from Westmoreland Manor. Lara was inspired to learn the game having discovered both her parents were keen golfers with low handicaps.

Oak Manor Club House

12th Green

5 October 1970

Lara arrived home from an indifferent game of golf; her putting had let her down badly. She took her golf clubs out of her new Triumph Stag and carried them into the townhouse. Just as she placed them under the stairs, she heard the telephone. She reached the receiver on the fifth ring.

'Hello, this is Lara.'

'Hi, Lars, it's Jane.'

'Hi, Jane how are you darling?'

'I'm afraid I have some sad news, Lars.'

Lara's heart sank, she'd heard those words before.

'What is it?'

'Janis died yesterday.'

'What! How?'

'Drug overdose.'

'Oh my God. I can't believe it! She was younger than me.'

'I thought I'd better call you before it hits the papers over there.'

'Yes, thank you, Jane, I appreciate it. This is so sad. They say bad news comes in threes. What with Jimmie Hendrix dying a few weeks ago and now this – I hope this is the end of it.'

'I'll speak to you again soon when I hear about the funeral arrangements.'

'OK, I'm not sure if I'll be able to make it, but I'll try.'

'Bye Lara, love you.'

'You too, Jane.'

Sundays were reserved for taking their magnificent Arabian mares out for a long ride. Lara's horse was named Rosie and Lisbeth's Angel Fire.

Lara asked Lisbeth if they could miss the ride as she was too upset about Janis's death.

Lara telephoned Jane on the following Tuesday as she had not heard from her.

'Hi Jane. It's Lara. Sorry to bother you, but I've decided I will fly over for the funeral. I need to know the date so I can arrange flights.'

'Hi, Lara I was going to phone you later today. I've been informed that it will be a private funeral with just family.'

'I can understand that however there would be plenty of us who would love to say the last goodbye to Pearl.'

'Well, Janis was true to her heart. She allocated $2,500 for a wake to be attended by her friends.'

'That's a lot of money for a party! It should be great.'

'So why don't you fly over? It's being held on the 26th at The Lion's Share in San Anselmo, about 20 miles from San Francisco.'

'Yes, I know it. I've seen a few groups play there, including Janis. What the fuck, why not. I'll let you know my flight details once I've booked them. Would you be able to pick me up?'

'Of course, I will. You can stay at my place or maybe you'd prefer to ask David Crosby if you can sleep in your house?'

'I think I'd rather stay with you although I'll probably go over and see how he's going.'

'OK, well let me know when you know what time you fly in. I'm looking forward to seeing you, babe.'

'Me too.'

Lara booked her tickets with British Airways first class. She was due to land in the afternoon of the 25th.

Jane picked Lara up at San Francisco Airport and drove home to her house in Haight-Ashbury. They both looked at Janis's house in silence; what was sorrowful was Janis's Porsche still parked outside the house.

'Somebody should move that into storage, or it will be stolen,' said Lara.

'Yeah, I suppose you're right. Although you'd never be able to drive it. It's got to be the most recognisable Porsche on the planet.'

'That's true.'

The two girlfriends caught up with each other's news and drank *Southern Comfort* in Pearl's memory. Finally, they went to bed.

Monday, 26 October

Jane and Lara woke late and ate breakfast on the Patio. Lara expressed a desire to go downtown and buy a new outfit for the wake, something she had done before the first date with David. The two women walked through Macys eventually finding something suitable: a pants suit designed by Ralph Lauren.

They ate a light lunch at a café in Union Square before heading back to Haight-Ashbury to get ready to attend Janis's wake.

Jane drove the 20 miles to San Anselmo where The Lion's Share, the venue selected by Janis, was located.

When the two friends arrived, they could see people carrying in cases of liquor and food.

The Lion's Share

At 7 pm the wake officially began. The *Southern Comfort* was flowing, as was the wine. Several trays of cookies were being passed around – unbeknownst to most of the party-goers they were hash cookies.

The Grateful Dead started up at about 9 pm and brought the house down, and then various other friends of Pearl's played, including the Mama and Papas.

Overall it was exactly what Janis would have wanted. Her contribution of $2,500 was well spent and enjoyed.

Jane and Lara left the party at midnight driving home to Jane's house. Lara visited David late the following morning, hoping he would have got over the wake by then. It took some knocking but they finally got a response although he looked well and truly hung over when he answered the door.

Lara had a quick look around the house and apart from his untidiness it was in good shape.

Jane drove Lara to the airport and before she knew it she was back in London 11 hours later. She was pleased she made the effort, not only for Janis, but to catch up with old friends, particularly Jane.

HOUSE OF LORDS

CHAPTER 25

Despite another loss, life was good for the young surgeon. Her work was satisfying and her weekdays at Kensington and weekends at Westmoreland were enjoyable.

However, she began to think about her heritage and the title she inherited from her father. Lara had never addressed herself as the countess, and very few people were aware of her social standing. She was more than mindful of the fact that her peerage entitled her to sit in the House of Lords.

She had become close to Graham Sutton. She not only admired him for his surgical skills but he had also become a confidant and advisor to the young surgeon.

Lara approached her mentor with the concept that she take up her hereditary right to become a member of The House of Lords.

'Apart from the prestige Lara, what is your motivation to become a member?'

'Graham I'm not interested in the prestige. If I were, I would have insisted on being addressed as countess long ago. I've thought I can make a difference. You know, to give something back to the country.'

'Yes, I can see your point. I suppose the good thing is you don't have to resign from the hospital unlike the House of Commons.'

'That's right, although there are going to be times when I'm required to sit in the house when I'm booked to operate. I think those instances would be minimal and hopefully rescheduling a patient's procedure would overcome the problem.'

'Have you sat in the visitor's gallery to get a feel for the place yet?'

'No, I intend to do so soon.'

'Well, that would be my advice. Attend a couple of sittings and then make your decision.'

'So I take it you'd still want me if I decided to go ahead?'

'I've always wanted you, Lara.'

'Graham. Behave!'

The next sitting of the House of Lord was scheduled for 1 March and Lara decided she would attend on the first day.

The Palace of Westminster where the House of Lords sat was a short taxi ride from her townhouse. She made her way to the visitor's gallery and waited in anticipation.

House of Lords Visitors Gallery

The members of the house began to file in and take their seats and Lara could not help but be impressed with the pageantry.

The Lord Speaker, the Lord Hailsham of Marylebone, was the last to take his seat in the speaker's chair. Once he was seated the other members took their seats.

The Lord Speaker was an experienced politician named Quinton Hogg. He had been a conservative Member of Parliament since 1938.

Hogg's father died in 1950 and Hogg entered the House of Lords as the 2nd Viscount Hailsham. Believing his political career to be over, he concentrated on the bar for some years, becoming head of his chambers, and did not at first hold office when the Conservatives returned to power in 1951. He became First Lord of the Admiralty under Eden in 1956, and under Macmillan was chairman of the party and campaign organiser for the 1959 general election.

In June 1963 when his fellow Minister John Profumo had to resign after admitting to telling lies to Parliament about his private life, Hogg attacked him savagely on television. Sir Reginald Paget called this 'a virtuoso performance of the art of kicking a friend in the guts'. He added, 'When self-indulgence has reduced a man to the shape of Lord Hailsham, sexual continence involves no more than a sense of the ridiculous'.

John Profumo

The Profumo affair was in British history, a political and intelligence scandal in the early 1960s that helped topple the Conservative Party government of Prime Minister Harold Macmillan. Involving sex, a Russian spy, and the secretary of state for war, the scandal captured the attention of the British public and discredited the government.

At a party at the country estate of Lord Astor on 8 July, 1961, British Secretary of State for War John Profumo, then a rising 46-year-old Conservative Party politician, was introduced to 19-year-old London dancer Christine Keeler by Stephen Ward, an osteopath with contacts in both the aristocracy and the underworld. Also, present at this gathering was a Russian military attaché, Eugene Ivanov, who was Keeler's lover.

Christine Keeler

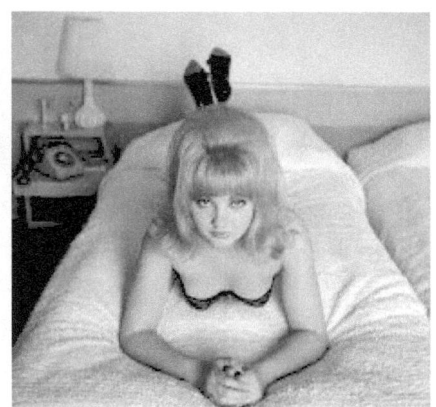

Mandy Rice-Davies

Through Ward's influence, Profumo began an affair with Keeler, and rumours of their involvement soon began to spread. In March 1963 Profumo lied about the affair to Parliament, stating that there was 'no impropriety whatsoever' in his relationship with Keeler. Evidence to the contrary quickly became too great to hide, however, and, 10 weeks later Profumo resigned, admitting 'with deep remorse' that he had deceived the House of Commons. Prime Minister Macmillan continued in office until October, but the scandal was pivotal in his eventual downfall, and within a year the opposition Labour Party defeated the Conservatives in a national election.

Despite charges of attempted espionage, neither the FBI, nor British intelligence was able to confirm or deny that Ivanov had attempted to entrap Profumo or to use Keeler as an access agent. Ivanov left Britain before the scandal became public, attending the Academy of the General Staff and later serving in important intelligence positions until his retirement in 1981.

Following her trial, in which she was convicted of perjury and conspiracy, Keeler sank into obscurity, though in 2001 she wrote an autobiography, which many considered an essentially worthless account of the affair. Ward committed suicide on the last day of his trial for pimping. Profumo began a career in philanthropy and was named Commander of the British Empire in 1975 for his charitable work.

1973

Abortion Legalised in America

Skylab America's First Space Station Launched

America withdraws from Vietnam

1 November 1 1973

Most of the debate in the House centred on the growing unemployment rate and the Heath Government's failing to curb it. Militant union activity was also hotly debated.

At the end of the day Lara decided she could make a contribution but not as a conservative or Labour member. She decided the cross bench was where she should sit.

The following week she gave notice to the Lord Speaker that she wished to take her seat in The House of Lords.

The young countess rang her dearest friend with the news.

'Hello Jane, it's the countess speaking.'

'The countess? My, aren't we being very regal today.'

'Well I have every right to be. I'm about to become a member of The House of Lords.'

'You're kidding me. Really?'

'I've decided I might be able to make a contribution to my once great country.'

'Lara that's fantastic! Won't you miss your work at the hospital?'

'No, I'll be able to continue on there. I can juggle both roles.'

'I can't wait to tell James. He won't believe it.'

'Well, actually the reason for my call is to invite you two to the opening of Parliament by the Queen. I'm entitled to invite family, but I don't have any. So you and James are the closest I have.'

'Lara, we'd be honoured. When is it?'

'February 3. By the way I'm shouting you both business class seats.'

'No you're not! We'll pay our own way – economy.'

'I won't let you come if you don't accept. Come on Jane, I can afford it. Let me do this for you both.'

'OK, you're being very generous.'

'Great! That's settled then. I'll arrange the tickets from this end.'

'See you in Parliament.'

'You will.'

1974

Patty Hearst Kidnapped

US President Richard Nixon Resigns

Halie Selassie, Emperor of Ethiopia, Deposed

3 February 1974

The Countess de Neville received notice that she was required to present herself to the Lord Great Chamberlain to be inducted with several other peers into the House of Lords at the Palace of Westminster. Her father Harold de Neville, Earl of Somerset, had never taken his seat in the chamber, although it had been his intention prior to his untimely death. The robes she wore to the short ceremony had belonged to her grandfather who had been a member for over thirty years.

Each new member was required to swear allegiance to the Queen.

I, Lara de Neville, Countess of Somerset swear by Almighty God that I will be faithful and bear true allegiance to Her Majesty Queen Elizabeth, her heirs and successors, according to law. So help me God.

The new inductees were handed a booklet outlining the rules of the house and the protocols to be followed. Lara, being an independent member, did not have the benefit of the party offering support and guidance – she was on her own.

Once sworn in, the new members were required to attend the opening of both houses in the afternoon.

There were time-honoured traditions to be followed, the first of these being:

Searching of the Cellars

The Yeomen of the Guard search the cellars of the Palace of Westminster to prevent a modern-day gunpowder plot. The plot of 1605 involved a failed attempt by English Catholics to blow up the Houses of Parliament and kill the Protestant King James 1 and the aristocracy. Since that year, the cellars have been searched, now largely, but not only, for ceremonial purposes.

Assembly of Peers and Commons

Lara and the other peers assembled in the House of Lords wearing their robes. Senior representatives of the judiciary and members of the diplomatic corps joined them. The Commons assembled in their own chamber, wearing ordinary day dress, and began the day, as any other, with prayers.

Delivery of Parliamentary Hostage

Before the Queen was to depart Buckingham Palace the Treasurer, Comptroller and Vice-Chamberlain of the Queen's Household delivered ceremonial white staves to her. The Queen kept the Vice-Chamberlain 'prisoner' for the duration of the state opening ensuring her safe return. The Vice-Chamberlain's imprisonment is now purely ceremonial, though he does remain under guard; originally, it guaranteed the safety of the Sovereign as he or she entered a possibly hostile Parliament. The tradition stems from the time of Charles1, who had a contentious relationship with Parliament and was eventually beheaded in 1649 during the Civil War between the monarchy and Parliament. A copy of Charles I's death warrant is displayed in the robing room used by the Queen as a ceremonial reminder of what can happen to a Monarch who attempts to interfere with Parliament.

Arrival of Royal Regalia

Before the arrival of the Queen, the Imperial State Crown is carried to the Palace of Westminster in its own state coach. From the Victoria Tower, the Queen's Barge Master passes the Crown to the Comptroller of the Lord Chamberlain's office. It is then carried, along with the Great Sword of State and the Cap of Maintenance, to be displayed in the Royal Gallery.

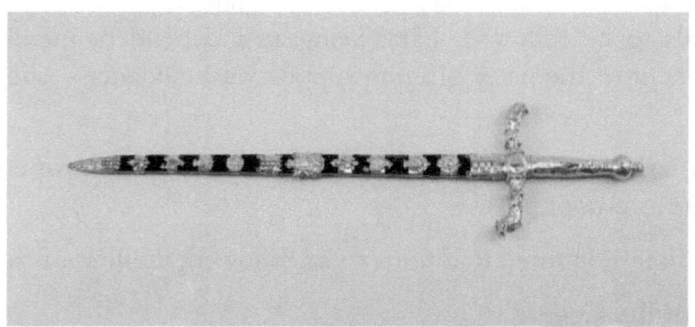

Great Sword of State

Cap of Maintenance

Arrival of the Sovereign and assembly of Parliament

The Queen arrived at the Palace of Westminster in a horse-drawn coach, entering through the Sovereign's Entrance under the Victoria Tower; she was accompanied by her consort The Duke of Edinburgh. Members of the armed forces lined the procession route from Buckingham Palace to the Palace of Westminster. The Royal Standard was hoisted to replace the Union Flag upon the Sovereign's entrance and remained flying whilst she was in attendance. She took on the Parliament Robe of State and Imperial State Crown in the Robing Chamber. The Queen then proceeded through the Royal Gallery to the House of Lords immediately preceded by the Earl Marshal, and by one peer carrying the Cap of Maintenance on a white rod, and another peer carrying the Great Sword of State, all followed the Lord Great Chamberlain and his white stick raised aloft. The Queen, sat on her throne, wearing the Imperial State Crown, and instructed the House saying, 'My Lords, pray be seated.' The Duke of Edinburgh took his seat on the throne to her left.

The Queen on Her Way to Open Parliament

Royal summons to the Commons

The Lord Great Chamberlain raised his wand of office to signal to the Gentleman Usher of the Black Rod to summon the members of the House of Commons. Black Rod, escorted by the Doorkeeper of the House of Lords and a police inspector, approached the doors to the Chamber of the Commons.

In 1642, King Charles 1 stormed into the House of Commons in an unsuccessful attempt to arrest the 'five members' which included the celebrated English patriot and leading parliamentarian, John Hampden. Since that time, no British monarch has entered the House of Commons when it is sitting.

As Black Rod approached, the doors were slammed shut symbolising the rights of Parliament and its independence from the Monarch. He struck with the end of his ceremonial staff three times on the closed doors of the Commons chamber, he was then admitted. At the bar, Black Rod bowed to the speaker before he proceeded to the dispatch box where he announced the command of the Monarch for the attendance of the Commons, in the following words:

'Mr Speaker, The Queen commands this honourable House to attend Her Majesty immediately in the House of Peers.'

Procession of the Commons

The Speaker proceeded to attend the summons at once. The Serjeant-at-Arms picked up the ceremonial mace and, with the Speaker and Black Rod, led the Members of the House of Commons walking, in pairs, towards the House of Lords. The Prime Minister and the Leader of the Opposition followed by The Deputy Prime Minister and the Deputy Leader of the Opposition walked side by side, leading the two lines of MPs. The Commons arrived at the Bar of the House of Lords and bowed to The Queen. No person who is not a member of the Upper House may pass the Bar unbidden when it is in session; a similar rule applies to the Commons. They remained standing at the Bar during the speech.

Delivery of the scroll

The Queen then read a prepared speech, known as the 'Speech from the Throne' or the 'Queen's Speech', outlining the Government's agenda for the coming year. The speech was written by the Prime Minister and his cabinet members, and reflected the legislative agenda for which the Government was seeking the agreement of both Houses of Parliament. It was traditionally written on goatskin vellum, and presented on bended knee for Her Majesty to read by the Lord Chancellor, who produces the scroll from a satchel-like bag. The Lord Chancellor walked backwards down the steps of the throne, continuing to face the monarch.

Delivery of the Speech

The speech was addressed to 'My Lords and Members of the House of Commons'.

The Queen read the entire speech in a neutral and formal tone, implying neither approval nor disapproval of the proposals of Her Majesty's Government: the Queen made constant references to 'My Government' when reading the text. After the Queen listed the main bills to be introduced during the session, she stated: 'other measures will be laid before you', thus leaving the Government scope to introduce bills not mentioned in the speech.

The Queen mentioned the Prince Consort of Denmark would be making a State visit.

She also mentioned Abdul Halim Sultan of Kedah Malaysia would be visiting.

The Queen concluded the speech by saying:

'My Lords and Members of the House of Commons, I pray that the blessing of Almighty God may rest upon your counsels'.

Departure of monarch

Following the speech, the Queen left the chamber before the Commons bowed again and returned to their Chamber.

Jane and James were enthralled by the ceremony. The closest they had been to anything even remotely similar was watching the Presidential inauguration on television.

Lara had arranged to meet her friends on the Parliamentary terrace fronting the River Thames. They would attend a cocktail party to celebrate the opening of Parliament.

'Thank you for inviting us Lara. It was absolutely amazing,' said Jane.

'Thank you for coming. It meant a lot to me.'

'Have you met any of the other peers as yet?'

'Not really, just the new boys and girls at the swearing in ceremony.'

'Have you got anything planned after the cocktail party?'

'I do. We're going to meet a few friends including Lisbeth and Graham the chief surgeon at the hospital at my favourite restaurant 'Simpson's in the Strand'. It's one of London's best having been established since1828.'

Lara and her two friends caught a taxi to Simpson's in the Strand where Lara had booked a table for eight.

The meal was superb, the wine was exceptional as was the company – overall a wonderful evening.

Lara was hoping Jane and James could extend their stay in London for a few more days but unfortunately Jane was about to defend a client accused of embezzlement; she needed to get back to San Francisco.

Lara's first full day of sitting in the House was 4 February, and news had reached the members of a major coach bombing on the M62, a 107-mile-long west-east trans-Pennine motorway in Northern England, connecting Liverpool and Hull via Manchester and Leeds.

The IRA had murdered eight British soldiers and four civilians.

The House of Lords expressed their disgust and offered their sympathy to the families of those lost.

17 June 17

Terror came to the Houses of Parliament when an IRA bomb exploded causing extensive damage and injuring eleven people.

5 October

The Guilford and Woolwich pub bombings killed four soldiers and a civilian and wounded 44 patrons.

22 October

A bomb planted by the Provisional IRA explodes in London injuring 3 people.

21 November

The Birmington pub bombings killed 21 and injured 182.

25 November

The Prevention of Terrorism (Temporary Provisions) Act 1974 was passed in the space of three days. The conception of the Bill was announced on 25 November 1974, when the Home Secretary, Roy Jenkins, warned that, 'The powers … are Draconian. In combination they are unprecedented in peacetime. I believe these are fully justified to meet the clear and present danger.' In response, Parliament was fanatically enthusiastic and had passed the Bill by 29 November, virtually without amendment or dissent.

Lara knew this madness must stop. It would become her major focus while sitting in The House of Lords.

GIVE IRELAND BACK TO THE IRISH

PAUL MCCARTNEY

CHAPTER 26

1975

Cambodian Genocide Begins

Civil War in Lebanon Begins

Microsoft Founded

January 1975

Lara's maiden speech focused on the Northern Ireland conflict in essence she argued:

'Lord Speaker, the age of Britain's colonialism is over. We as a nation now recognise that the dominance of one country over another is morally wrong; the Irish people controlled Ireland before we invaded. The Irish argue they have a right to the ownership of their land because they were the ones who cultivated and nourished it. The use of force to seize that land from the people's control was unjust. They had no choice but to hand over their land – it was forced upon them.

'It is up to us to right this historical wrong. I believe Lord Speaker that Britain should relinquish Northern Ireland.'

The Countess de Neville's speech was widely reported in newspapers across Great Britain with a mixed response.

The day after Lara's maiden speech in the house a Labour member approached her.

'Countess de Neville I was very impressed with your speech yesterday.'

'Thank you Lord Duffy. I'm glad you liked it.'

'Your views are very much in line with mine and the faction I am associated with.'

'You mean the extreme left wing with an alliance to the IRA?'

'No, we don't have an alliance with the IRA, although we do sympathise with their cause.'

'I see.'

'May I ask you why you chose to sit on the cross bench?'

'It gives me the flexibility I desire. I can vote on a bill based on its merits not what the party stipulates.'

'That's true, although you do miss out on the strength of numbers that belonging to a party brings.'

'That's a sacrifice I'm willing to make.'

'Well Countess, if you ever change your mind the Labour party would welcome you with open arms.'

'Thank you Lord Duffy. And please call me Lara.'

'I will. And you can call me Colin.'

The two members parted ways, both impressed with one another.

Lara continued to make her views known inside and outside the House and as the year progressed more and more violence occurred.

On 31 July at Buskhill outside Newry the Miami Showband, a very popular cabaret act, was returning home to Dublin having completed a show in Banbridge. Members of the Ulster Voluntary Force (UVF) wearing stolen British Army uniforms ambushed them at a bogus roadside checkpoint on the A1 road. Three band members were shot and killed while two UVF fighters were killed when a bomb they had loaded into the band's mini bus exploded prematurely.

The Miami Showband

1976

Apple Computer Founded

Nadia Comaneci Given Seven Perfect Tens

North and South Vietnam Join to Form the Socialist Republic of Vietnam

January 1976

Eleven Protestant workers were murdered in South Armagh after having been ordered off their bus by an IRA gang and shot in cold blood. One survived despite having received 18 bullet wounds.

The IRA claimed the shootings were in retaliation for murders of two Catholic families the previous night.

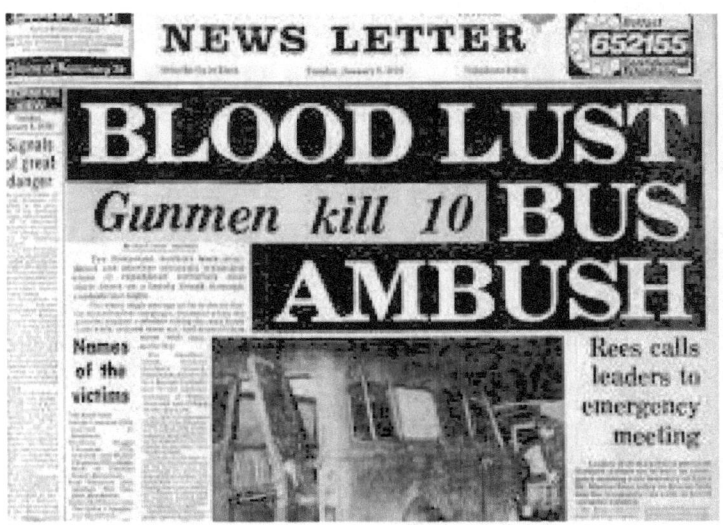

There were other major issues debated in Parliament including borrowing money from the International Monetary Fund (IMF).

September 1976

Britain is forced to borrow money from the International Monetary Fund.

A crisis in sterling forced the Labour government to turn to the International Monetary Fund (IMF), making Britain the first major Western state to be forced into this humiliating course of action. In return for the loan, the IMF demanded cuts in government spending. After a political battle within the British government, the IMF terms were accepted and imposed in December.

Lara voted in favour of the budgetary cuts in order for Britain to survive her monetary crisis.

1978/79

John Paul II Becomes Pope

Iran Takes American Hostages in Tehran

Mother Teresa Awarded the Nobel Peace Prize

Winter 1978/79

Lara decided she needed to get out of England for a while. Her workload had been intense; she felt a holiday abroad was in order. She had been going out with a charming man, Lawrence Windsor an art dealer. His gallery, Elite Art in Mayfair, was regarded as one of London's best.

The couple was eating dinner at Charlotte's Bistro, a small intimate restaurant with an excellent reputation.

'Lawrence do you think it would be within the realms of possibility that you could get away from the gallery for a couple of weeks?'

'Possibly darling, why do you ask?'

'I've decided to go skiing at St Moritz for ten days or so. I'd love it if you accompanied me.'

'I'd love to Lara. When are you thinking of going?'

'I took the liberty of booking our airfares departing on 15 January. I've also booked a suite at the Carlton Hotel.'

'You don't muck about do you, my love. Well, how could I say no?'

'That's excellent! By the way, you do ski don't you?'

'I do. Black runs preferred.'

'Really? Well, I'll try to keep up with you, darling.'

Lawrence picked Lara up from her townhouse at 9 am and drove to Heathrow. The Range Rover had no difficulty fitting the skis, boot bag and suitcases in the luggage compartment.

'I haven't asked you what airline we're flying on. Lars I need to know what car park to use.'

'You need to drive to the VIP terminal. We're flying with Private Fly.'

'You mean you booked a private jet?'

'I did. It's easier.'

'You never cease to amaze me, Countess.'

'Well, I don't get the opportunity too often, so why not splash out when you can?'

Lawrence parked the car in the VIP valet car park. An employee of Private Fly took their luggage then drove the Range Rover to the long-term car park.

Lara and Lawrence checked in then took a seat in the luxury lounge and waited to be chauffeured to their plane.

It wasn't long before the Rolls pulled up outside the lounge to take the couple to their private jet. Lawrence felt like James Bond getting out of the limousine and climbing the steps of the Cessna Mustang.

The jet taxied out to the runway and they were now on their way to a fantastic holiday. The flight took an hour and forty-five minutes before landing at Engadin airport where a hotel limousine met them and drove them to the Carlton fifteen minutes away.

The Carlton Hotel St Moritz

The next twelve days were filled with skiing in magnificent conditions, eating wonderful food and making love every night. Unfortunately, all good things must come to an end. Lara needed to return to London for the next sitting of the House of Lords while Lawrence needed to get back to the gallery.

It was a holiday neither of them would forget.

Lara returned to the chaos being experienced in Great Britain.

Strikes paralysed Britain during the so-called 'Winter of Discontent'.

Hospital ancillary staff, ambulance men and dustmen went on strike following industrial action by petrol tanker and lorry drivers. Hospitals were picketed, the dead left unburied, and troops called in to control rats swarming around heaps of uncollected rubbish. The large number of simultaneous strikes, the violence and perceived mean-mindedness of the picketing (which included the turning away of ambulances) created a sense of alarm in the electorate about the decline of British society.

Lara was becoming more and more alarmed with what was taking place in Britain. She knew her one vote would not make much difference.

Her life outside the House of Lords was more satisfying. She continued her reconstructive plastic surgery at the London Free Hospital where she was now head of Department. Dr Graham Sutton had accepted a teaching professorship, ironically at the John Hopkins Hospital in San Francisco where Lara completed her internship.

Lara had made friends both inside and outside the Parliament and therefore had a full and satisfying social life.

Her love life was interesting if unusual. She was constantly asked out for dinner and such and in some cases she would let the relationship flourish to the point where she and her suitor would have sex. As soon as Lara felt things were getting too serious she would terminate the affair.

That point had arrived with Lawrence. Despite the fact she had strong feelings for him she decided the relationship must end.

She telephoned him and gave him the news. He was devastated; he had visions of marrying Lara some time in the near future.

Sub-consciously she erected a barrier protecting her from the hurt she had suffered in the past.

In 1979 an event happened which made her decide it was time to run for a seat in the Lower House.

27 August 1979

Lord Mountbatten's Assassination.

Lord Mountbatten and Family Aboard *Shadow V*

Lord Mountbatten usually holidayed at his summer home, Classiebawn Castle, in Mullaghmore, a small seaside village in County Sligo, Ireland. The village was only 12 miles from the border with Northern Ireland. In 1978, the IRA had allegedly attempted to shoot Mountbatten as he was aboard his boat, but choppy seas had prevented the sniper lining up his target accurately.

Despite security advice and warnings from the Irish police, on 27 August 1979, Mountbatten went lobster potting and tuna fishing in his 30-foot wooden boat, Shadow V, which had been moored in the harbour at Mullaghmore. IRA operative, Thomas McMahon, had slipped onto the unguarded boat that night and attached a radio-controlled bomb weighing 50 pounds. With Mountbatten aboard, just a few hundred yards from the shore, the bomb was detonated. The force of the blast destroyed the vessel; Mountbatten's legs were almost blown off. Local fishermen pulled Lord Mountbatten, alive from the water; however, he died from his injuries before arriving back at the shore. Also aboard the boat were his eldest daughter Patricia (Lady Brabourne), her husband John (Lord Brabourne), their twin sons Nicholas and Timothy, John's mother Doreen, Lady Brabourne, and Paul Maxwell, a young crew member from County Fermanagh. Nicholas aged 14, and Paul aged 15 were killed by the blast and the others were seriously injured. Lady Brabourne aged 83 died from her injuries the following day.

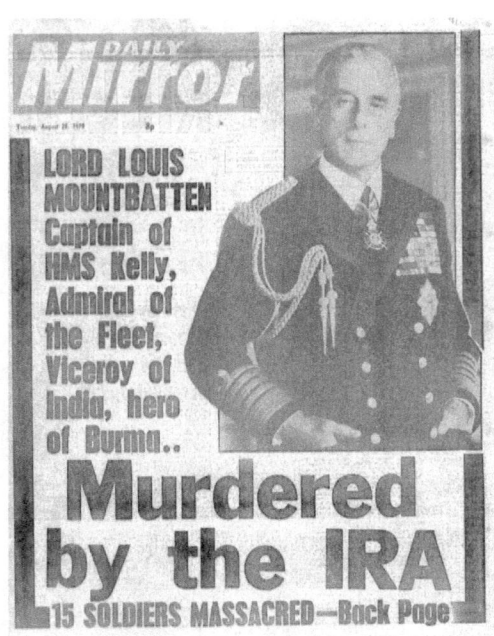

The IRA issued a statement afterward, saying:

The IRA claim responsibility for the execution of Lord Louis Mountbatten. This operation is one of the discriminate ways we can bring to the attention of the English people the continuing occupation of our country. The death of Mountbatten and the tributes paid to him will be seen in sharp contrast to the apathy of the British government and the English people to the deaths of over three hundred British soldiers, and the deaths of Irish men, women and children at the hands of their forces.

Six weeks later, Sinn Féin vice-president Gerry Adams said of Mountbatten's death:

The IRA gave clear reasons for the execution. I think it is unfortunate that anyone has to be killed, but the furore created by Mountbatten's death showed up the hypocritical attitude of the media establishment. As a member of the House of Lords, Mountbatten was an emotional figure in both British and Irish politics. What the IRA did to him is what Mountbatten had been doing all his life to other people; and with his war record I don't think he could have objected to dying in what was clearly a war situation. He knew the danger involved in coming to this country. In my opinion, the IRA achieved its objective: people started paying attention to what was happening in Ireland.

Lord Mountbatten had introduced himself to Lara following her maiden speech and although he didn't agree with the sentiment, congratulated her on her overall presentation. Lord Mountbatten became an adviser and friend over the following years. Lara was devastated when she learnt of his murder along with members of his family.

This horrific event became the catalyst for her decision to relinquish her peerage and sit for a seat in The House of Commons.

Her next decision was which party to join: both the Conservatives and Labour had approached her over the years to join their party. An election was due to be held that year and Mr Callaghan was being tipped to lose to Margaret Thatcher. Lara was very much middle of the road. If she joined the Conservatives she would be labelled a left wing member; on the other hand Labour would label her right wing. She asked for advice from a number of people, including Lisbeth her long time friend and confidant. She also confided in Graham Sutton and Jane.

Finally she decided to join the Labour party on the basis she could make her mark in a party in opposition, looking for new blood and fresh ideas after what looked like it would be a heavy defeat. Another deciding factor was the Labour member for Taunton in Somerset had resigned from politics.

Lara was no longer Countess of Somerset; she was now just plain old Lara de Neville.

Lara won the pre-selection battle and campaigned hard. As predicted, Thatcher's Government won 339 seats, Labour won 69 and the Liberals 11.

Lara won her seat comfortably.

THE IRON LADY
VERSUS
THE FLOWER CHILD

CHAPTER 27

May 1979

James Callaghan was sitting in the Leader of the Opposition's office, a place he was unfamiliar with. He knew in his heart of hearts that he wouldn't be around for too much longer. He had been Prime Minister for three years as well as Chancellor of the Exchequer, Home Secretary and Foreign Secretary over the previous ten years. He began his parliamentary career 1945. That was long enough for any one, he thought.

He also knew that his successor would pick their own team so he made no changes to the cabinet he took to the election, even though it was now a shadow cabinet.

Although Lara had five years experience as a member of the House of Lords she knew she would be on a fast learning curve in her new role and new environment. Her time in the upper house was spent as an independent and now she was part of a large team with various factions.

Thatcher Economics

The Thatcher Government's first priority when taking government was to get inflation under control, sacrificing employment as its main objective.

The first step in achieving lower inflation was to increase interest rates to slow down the growth of the money supply and as a result lower inflation.

Margaret Thatcher preferred indirect taxation as opposed to income tax; she increased the VAT to 15 per cent, which resulted in a short-term rise in inflation.

Her monetary policy combined with the North Sea effect appreciated the English Pound, which had an adverse effect on business, particularly manufacturing. The number of unemployed increased to two million by the autumn of 1980, an increase of 500,000 over the number she inherited in 1979.

The Labour party was outraged and demanded Thatcher's priority should be to reduce unemployment. Their argument fell on deaf ears.

Even former Prime Minister Edward Heath, Margaret Thatcher's predecessor, became a harsh critic of Thatcher's economic policies. She dismissed his criticisms as sour grapes for taking his job.

She wasn't turning back and in the 1981 budget, ignoring an open letter by 364 economists; she increased taxes despite the recession.

1981

Assassination Attempt on Ronald Reagan

Assassination Attempt on the Pope

Prince Charles and Lady Dianna Spencer Marry

10 & 12 April

Brixton Riot

Brixton in South London was an area with chronic social and economic problems. Britain was in the middle of a recession in 1981, with the majority of the population suffering unknown hardships; however the black community was worse off than most with crippling unemployment, poor housing and a high crime rate.

Preceding the riot there had been growing tensions between the police and the inhabitants of Brixton. Several black youths died in a house fire during a party. The black community accused the police of not pursuing the perpetrators, blaming the tragedy on racial hatred. Subsequent investigations proved it had been an accident.

Darcus Howe was a black activist who organised a march called 'Black People's Day of Action'. It was estimated 25,000 people marched 17 miles from Brixton to Hyde Park passing the Houses of Parliament.

There were some skirmishes between police and marchers, but overall it was a peaceful demonstration.

The *Evening Standard* posted a front-page headline including a photo of a bloodied policeman next to a quote from Howe referring to the march as 'a good day'.

In early April the Metropolitan Police began Operation Swamp to reduce crime in the Brixton area, using the powers of the Vagrancy Act they stopped and searched nearly 1000 people arresting 82 over just five days. The black community claimed the police were disproportionately targeting black people.

10 April

A young police constable was walking his beat when he noticed a black youth, Michael Bailey, running towards him. He was apparently fleeing from three black youths. The policeman stopped Bailey and found he was bleeding badly, but the youth broke away from the constable. He was pursued and stopped again and it was discovered that Bailey had a 4-inch stab wound. Initially, Bailey was placed in a taxi to take him to hospital but later he was transferred to a police car to ensure he arrived at hospital more quickly. A police office bound his wound to try and stem the bleeding. Before the police car could begin its critical journey, about 50 youths surrounded the car shouting for Bailey's release and accusing the police of trying to kill him. The mob wrenched opened the door and pulled the injured youth out. They placed him in another vehicle with the intention of taking him to hospital. They told the officers, 'Let us look after our own'.

Rumours spread that the police had left Bailey to die; over 200 black youths turned on the police. The police response was to ramp up Operation Swamp arresting a further 81 blacks in the Railton Road area.

11–12 April

The news spread within the local community that Bailey had died as a result of police brutality, which fuelled tensions throughout the day and crowds began to gather.

In the afternoon around 4 pm two police officers stopped and searched a mini-cab in Railton Road. This action caused resentment amongst the crowd. At the same time Brixton Road was populated with an angry mob that began to pelt the police with rocks and bricks. The situation became more and more violent by 9 pm and 46 police officers had been injured five of them seriously. Shops were being looted throughout the district. The first fire began just after 6 pm. A police van had been set alight by rioters in Railton Road. The Fire Brigade were called and responded immediately. They were directed down to the end of Railton Road. Without warning, as they approached the fire over 300 rioters pelted them with rocks and bottles.

A call went out to all police officers across London for immediate assistance. There was no real strategy to stem the riot and the officers were not allocated appropriate riot gear. To make matters worse, police radio communication was proving to be difficult.

As the police began to move forward the rioters hurled bricks, bottles and Molotov Cocktails, slowing down the police advance.

As the night progressed, so to did the violence. By 8 pm two pubs, 26 businesses, several schools and various other buildings were burning out of control. Hundreds of local residents were trapped in their houses, too afraid to venture out.

By 9.30 pm over 1000 police were dispatched to Brixton. They managed to quell the riot and by Sunday morning 2500 police were in the Brixton area. It was only then that the Fire Brigade agreed to return.

The Aftermath

During the riot 299 police and over 65 members of the public were injured. More than 60 private vehicles and 56 police vehicles were totally destroyed. Over 30 buildings were burnt to the ground and a further 117 damaged.
The police arrested 82 rioters.

Scarman Report

The Home Secretary, William Whitelaw commissioned a public inquiry into the riot, headed by Lord Scarman.

Scarman found unquestionable evidence of the disproportionate and indiscriminate use of 'stop and search' powers by the police against black people. As a consequence, a new code for police behaviour was put forward in the *Police and Criminal Evidence Act 1984*; and the act also created an independent Police Complaints Authority, established in 1985, to attempt to restore public confidence in the force. Scarman concluded that 'complex political, social and economic factors created a disposition towards violent protest'.

Margaret Thatcher's Response

On 13 April, Margaret Thatcher dismissed the notion that unemployment and racism lay beneath the Brixton disturbances claiming, 'Nothing, but nothing, justifies what happened' – although figures showed high unemployment amongst Brixton's black population. Overall unemployment in Brixton stood at 13 percent, with 25.4 percent for ethnic minorities. Unemployment among black youths was estimated at 55 percent. Rejecting increased investment in Britain's inner cities, Thatcher added, 'Money cannot buy either trust or racial harmony.'

Lambeth London Borough Council leader, Ted Knight, complained that the police presence 'amounted to an army of occupation' that provoked the riots. Thatcher responded, 'what absolute nonsense and what an appalling remark ... No one should condone violence. No one should condone the events ... They were criminal, criminal.'

Michael Callaghan resigned eighteen months after the riots in November 1980. A left wing member was elected in his place his name was Michael Foot. He formed his Shadow Cabinet soon after his election; the new Shadow Minister for Health was Lara de Neville.

This is what Lara had been hoping for: an opportunity to make a difference. She was aware that her right wing views could clash with Foot's left wing philosophy. However, she knew she would be able to work within the party framework.

Where Lara differed philosophically with Foot centred on nuclear disarmament and withdrawal from the EEC. She respected his experience as a Parliamentarian – after all he was first elected in 1945 – but she disagreed with some of his policies.

Lara was walking to the House of Commons when she encountered the Prime Minister and her entourage. Mrs Thatcher stopped and engaged Lara in a conversation.

'Congratulations on your appointment as Shadow Health Minister, Lara.'

'Thank you, Prime Minister.'

'If only you had joined our side you could have been Minister for Health.'

'What can I say?'

'Not much.'

The Prime Minister and her group continued on their way, as did Lara.

Iranian Embassy Siege

Margaret Thatcher demonstrated her steel in 1980 when the Iranian Embassy in Princess Gate London was taken over by armed terrorists.

She authorised the SAS to use lethal force, the first time in 70 years it had been used on the British mainland.

The 6 terrorists held 26 hostages for six days until the SAS brought the siege to a dramatic conclusion, raiding the embassy and freeing the hostages. The raid was televised live and supported by the public.

Thatcher was applauded for her decisiveness and resolute approach to the siege. This was the first demonstration, of how she earned the reputation as the 'Iron Lady'

Lara, and her colleagues also applauded the Prime Minister and the SAS on the way the crisis was solved.

Storming the Embassy

Northern Island

The day before Thatcher was due to meet the Irish Taoiseach (Prime Minister) to discuss Northern Ireland, she announced in the House of Commons 'that the future of the constitutional affairs of Northern Ireland is a matter of Northern Ireland, this Government, this Parliament and no one else.'

In 1981 a number of IRA prisoners in Maze Prison (Long Kesh) went on a hunger strike to regain their status as political prisoners, which had been revoked five years earlier under the previous Labour Government.

One prisoner, Bobby Sands, was elected to the Parliament representing Fermanagh and South Tyrone. He died from starvation a few weeks later.

Margaret Thatcher refused their request declaring 'crime is crime is crime; it is not political.' Nine more prisoners died before most of their rights were restored; however Thatcher refused official recognition of their political status.

Lara de Neville argued strongly in Parliament that all IRA prisoners should be recognised as political prisoners.

She also was a strong opponent of Ulsterisation, despite it being introduced by the previous Labour Government. The policy was that Unionists of Northern Ireland should be at the forefront in combating Irish republicanism.

This would result in relieving the burden on the mainstream British Army and would elevate the role of the Ulster Defence Regiment and the Royal Ulster Constabulary.

1982

King Henry VIII's Ship the *Mary Rose* Raised After 437 Years

Reverend Sun Myung Moon Marries 2,075 Couples at Madison Square Garden

Vietnam War Memorial Opened in Washington, DC

Falkland War

2 April 1982

Argentina invaded the Falkland Islands and South Georgia, a British territory. Argentina had laid claim to the territory since 1810. The following day Margaret Thatched dispatched a naval task force in support of diplomatic efforts. If these failed, she would use force to evict the invaders.

Diplomacy failed and an amphibious and ground combat operation began. Thatcher knew she had overwhelming support from the British people.

After a short but bitter war Argentina surrendered on 14 June. It was a convincing win, however Britain suffered 258 casualties.

Victory brought a wave of patriotic enthusiasm and increased support for the Thatcher Government, with *Newsweek* declaring, 'The Empire Strikes Back'. One poll suggested that 84 per cent of the electorate approved of the prime minister's handling of the crisis.

Lara knew she would be Shadow Minister for Health for quite some time. Thatcher wasn't going anywhere.

The Labour member for Taunton was kept busy in her shadow health portfolio although Thatcher's Government was regarded as being effective in managing the National Health Service.

Lara made an annual trip to the United States to meet up with her lifelong friend Jane and her husband James. The couple no longer lived in Haight-Ashbury. They elevated their standing to Pacific Heights, one of the most expensive areas in San Francisco.

Jane's and James' Mansion

The two lawyers had left their firm, Orrik & Co, some years ago, starting up their own practice specialising in commercial law. The company now employed in excess of 100 people.

Lara always enjoyed her time in San Francisco. She still owned the house she had lived in with David and visited the tenants whenever she was in town.

She enjoyed visiting Haight-Ashbury, although it had changed since the mid-sixties when she lived there.

Lara revelled in the dinner table discussions comparing Thatcher to Regan. The two world leaders had very similar views, particularly in economics. She was very right of centre of the Labour Party, acknowledging the tough medicine being dispensed by both leaders was necessary. This opinion was not freely discussed with her party colleagues back home.

The Thatcher Government was well and truly entrenched in running the United Kingdom. The Iron Lady was earning her reputation as a tough leader who didn't take prisoners.

European integration

At Bruges, Belgium, in 1988, Thatcher made a speech in which she outlined her opposition to proposals from the European Community for a federal structure and increasing centralisation of decision-making. Although she had supported British membership, Thatcher believed that the role of the EC should be limited to ensuring free trade and effective competition, and feared that new EC regulations would reverse the changes she was making in the UK:

Poll Tax

Thatcher sought to relieve what she considered the unfair burden of property tax on the property-owning section of the population, and outlined a fundamental solution as her flagship policy in the Conservative manifesto for the 1987 election. Local government rates were replaced by the community charge, popularly known as the 'poll tax', which levied a flat rate on all adult residents. This proved unpopular, as lower earners would pay a much greater portion of their income in poll tax than higher earners –it would heavily redistribute the tax burden onto the less well off.

An indication of the unpopularity of the policy was given by a Gallup poll in March 1990 that put Labour 18.5 points ahead.

Thatcher's introduction of the Poll tax, her Government's perceived mishandling of the economy (in particular the high-interest rates of 15 per cent that eroded her support among homeowners and business people), and the divisions opening in the Conservative Party over European integration made her seem increasingly politically vulnerable and her party increasingly divided.

On 1 November 1990, Sir Geoffrey Howe, one of Thatcher's oldest and staunchest supporters, resigned from his position as Deputy Prime Minister in protest at Thatcher's European policy.

Her former cabinet colleague Michael Heseltine subsequently challenged her for the leadership of the party.

Thatcher decided, after consulting with her Cabinet colleagues, to withdraw from the contest. On 22 November, just after 9.30 am, she announced to the Cabinet that she would not be a candidate. Shortly afterwards, her staff made public what was, in effect, her resignation statement:

'Having consulted widely among my colleagues, I have concluded that the unity of the Party and the prospects of victory in a General Election would be better served if I stood down to enable Cabinet colleagues to enter the ballot for the leadership. I should like to thank all those in Cabinet and outside who have given me such dedicated support.'

She supported John Major as her successor and he duly won the leadership contest.

So ended the Thatcher era.

NEW LABOUR

CHAPTER 28

1994

Channel Tunnel Opens, Connecting Britain and France

Nelson Mandela Elected President of South Africa

Rwandan Genocide

Lara served under several leaders during Labour's term in opposition, initially as Shadow Minister for Health under Michael Foot and Neil Kinnock.

She was promoted to Shadow Foreign Secretary when John Smith was appointed Opposition Leader.

December 1994

The Prime Minister asked Lara to undergo a fact-finding tour to Australia, New Zealand and South East Asia to determine their attitudes towards China's changing role in the region.

In 1994 China's leaders proclaimed a period of comprehensive reforms, but these were not apparent at year's end apart from the introduction of a new tax system. Two conflicting images of China emerged. The first was that of a rapidly developing economic powerhouse, playing an increasingly important international role and vigorously asserting its interests on the stage of Asian and world politics. The second was that of a country with decreasing internal cohesion, beset by intractable social and economic problems and indifferently governed by the Communist Party veterans who were only interested in staying in power. The available evidence supported both of these images. China seemed a country not sure of its destination.

Tony Blair became Labour Leader in July 1994. He recognised Lara's abilities, appointing her Shadow Home Secretary.

Lara and her fellow shadow ministers at last felt confident they would attain the high office of Government. Tony Blair was an innovate leader with a fresh approach. His popularity in the polls kept rising as John Major's kept falling. It became obvious to all that Britain would have Labour Government after the 1997 election.

Lara made Australia her first port of call, meeting with the Prime Minister Paul Keating and his Minister for Foreign Affairs, Gareth Evans.

Keating saw his country as an integral part of Asia and in 1994 he continued his regular meetings in APEC countries, visiting Laos, Thailand and Vietnam in April, and Indonesia in June. He saw these countries as strategically significant to Australia – a security buffer to the vast and powerful People's Republic of China.

Lara used her time in Australia to visit Sydney and Melbourne. She hadn't been in the country before despite having friends living there.

She met up with an old friend of David's who had migrated to Sydney in 1978: George Wilson, who had been a roadie for Jefferson Airplane at the same time as David worked for Big Brother. George had met an Australian girl in San Francisco and fallen in love. He also fell in love with Australia; the country had been good to him. George now owned his own music company, as well as a promotions company.

Lara caught a taxi to George's and Jenny's house at a place called Double Bay and when the taxi pulled up outside the address Lara had given him she was impressed.

She paid the taxi-driver and walked up to the front veranda. The front door opened before she could ring the bell. George was standing there looking almost the same as he did all those years ago.

'Lara, you look great babe, come on in.'

'Hello George, you're looking pretty good yourself. I see you still have long hair and those boyish good looks.'

'It's the industry I'm in. You've got to look the part.'

'Where's Jenny? I'm looking forward to seeing her.'

'In the kitchen, where she should be.'

'Careful George!'

'Just kidding. Come on, I'll take you through.'

'Hello, Jenny. You look great!'

'Hi Lara, thanks hon. As good as I can with a husband and three children to manage.'

'Three, you have been busy. What ages?'

'Jade is 18, Jason is 16, and Kate is 10. Kate's the one we didn't think we'd have, but she's gorgeous.'

'So life is good for you all?'

'We've had our moments, but yes, life has turned out pretty well.'

'Enough chit-chat ladies! Would like a sparkling white to begin?'

Both women agreed it would be a pleasant start to the evening.

They sat out on the veranda overlooking Double Bay and Sydney Harbour beyond.

All three Wilson children came out and were introduced before they retreated to the television room to watch 'Friends'.

The three friends moved into the dining room where Jenny had laid a beautiful table.

'So Lars, you're an MP in the House of Commons. That must be interesting?' said George.

'Yes interesting, boring, exciting amazing and daunting all in one.'

'What made you decide to go into politics, Lara?' asked Jenny.

'I suppose I wanted to make a difference.'

'So what brings you to our fair shores?' asked George.

'I'm Shadow Foreign Minister. I need to touch base with the leaders of our allies around the world.'

'So I take it you've met with our Prime Minister?'

'Yes, yesterday in Canberra. Along with the Foreign Minister.'

'What was your impression of our illustrious leader?' asked George.

'Paul Keating is an impressive man. No doubt he has a massive intellect. He has a keen wit too.'

'You liked him?'

'Yes George, I did.'

'What about Gareth?'

'Not in the same class as Paul, but nevertheless impressive.'

'So where are you going when you depart from here Lara?' asked Jenny.

'I'm heading for New Zealand to meet with Jim Bolger and Don McKinnon.'

'Then home to Blighty?'

'Goodness no! Next will be Singapore and finally Malaysia. So that's enough about me. What about you two?'

'George developed a very successful touring company called Back Street Touring Company,' said Jenny.

'That's fantastic, George. Any names I should know?'

'The Rolling Stones in 92, Fleetwood Mac in 90, Dire Straits and a whole lot more including AC/DC.'

'George that's amazing! If David was alive, he'd be envious.'

'I know what you've been up to, Jenny. Raising three kids no doubt.'

'Yeah, although I do the books for George and lend a hand when he's got a big tour happening. Do you mind if I ask you a personal question, Lara?'

'Go ahead. Not sure if I'll answer it.'

'Why haven't you ever married?' asked Jenny.

'I suppose I haven't met the right man. If David had lived there would be doubt we would have married, however.'

'Do you get lonely?'

'Not really. Don't get me wrong. I've been in plenty of relationships. Just none where I felt I wanted to marry the fellow. I have enough in my life to ensure I don't get lonely.'

The evening ended at midnight, George telephoned for a taxi to take Lara back to the Hilton. Her plane departed for New Zealand at eight the next morning.

The trip was very successful and she flew home to report to John Smith and his cabinet.

1997

First *Harry Potter* Book Is Released

Hong Kong Returned to China

Princess Dianna Killed in a Car Crash

The results were:

Leader	Tony Blair	John Major	Paddy Ashdown
Party	Labour	Conservative	Liberal Democrat
Leader since	July 1994	November 1990	July 1988
Leader's seat	Sedgefield	Huntingdon	Yeovil
Last election	271 seats, 34.4%	336 seats, 41.9%	20 seats, 17.8%
Seats before	273	343	18
Seats won	418	165	46
Seat change	+145*	-178*	+28*
Popular vote	13,518,167	9,600,943	5,242,947
Percentage	43.2%	30.7%	16.8%
Swing	+8.8	-11.2	-1.0

The Home Secretary is responsible for the internal affairs of England and Wales, and for immigration and citizenship for the United Kingdom. The remit of the Home Office also includes policing in England and Wales and matters of national security, as the Security Service, MI5, is directly accountable to the Home Secretary. The Home Secretary is also the minister responsible for prisons and probation in England and Wales.

1997 nationalist riots in Northern Ireland

Tony Blair and his cabinet hardly had time to settle into their new offices, having won the 1997 election in May, when trouble raised its ugly head in Northern Ireland once again.

From 6 to 11 July there were mass protests, fierce riots and gun battles in Irish nationalist districts of Northern Ireland. Irish nationalists/republicans, in some cases supported by the IRA, attacked the Royal Ulster Constabulary aka RUC and the British Army. The protests and violence were sparked by the decision to allow the Orange Order; a Protestant, unionist organisation, to march through a Catholic/nationalist neighbourhood of Portadown. Irish nationalists were outraged by the decision and by the RUC's aggressive treatment of those protesting against the march. There had been a bitter dispute over the march for many years.

Several members of the Loyalist Volunteer Force aka LVF were meeting in the house belonging to Billy Wright.

The Loyalist Volunteer Force was a small Ulster loyalist paramilitary group in Northern Ireland. It was established by Billy Wright in 1996 when he and his unit split from the Ulster Volunteer Force (UVF) after breaking its ceasefire. They had belonged to the UVF's Mid-Ulster Brigade and Wright had been the brigade's commander. In a two-year period from August 1996, the LVF waged a paramilitary campaign with the stated goal of combating Irish republicanism. During this time, it killed at least 14 people in gun and bomb attacks. Almost all of its victims were Catholic civilians who were killed at random.

'What are we going to do with that bitch Lara de Neville she's so far up the IRA's arse it's not fucking funny. If she has her way the British will be pulling out of Northern Ireland by Christmas,' said Michael O'Meara.

'She's the one who has the cops reporting to her. You watch when we march through Drumcree. The bitch will be ordering the bastards to shoot as many Protestants as they bloody well can,' said Billy.

'Well, all I know is something should be done about her.'

The security forces were attacked hundreds of times by rioters throwing stones and petrol bombs, and by IRA members with rifles and grenades. The RUC and British Army fired more than 2,500 plastic bullets at rioters and exchanged gunfire with the IRA. More than 100 civilians and 65 security force personnel were injured. There were many complaints of police brutality; a 13-

year-old boy went into a coma after being shot in the head by a plastic bullet. Hundreds of burning vehicles were used to block roads. The security forces had to withdraw entirely from some nationalist areas of Belfast.

The Orange Order is a Protestant, unionist fraternal organisation. It insists that it should be allowed to march its traditional route to-and-from Drumcree Church each July. It had marched this route since 1807, when the area was mostly farmland. However, today most of this route is through the mainly Catholic/Irish nationalist part of Portadown. The residents sought to re-route the march away from their area, seeing it as 'triumphalist'and 'supremacist'. They likened it to a Ku Klux Klan march through an African-American neighbourhood.

On 18 June 1997 Alistair Graham, Chairman of the Parades Commission warned after the killing of two RUC officers in nearby Lurgan that the IRA was seeking to raise tensions before the march so that a compromise would be impossible. In June 1997, Secretary of State, Mo Mowlam had privately decided to let the march proceed. However, in the days leading up to the march, she insisted that no decision had been made. She met Taioseach Bertie Ahern, who stressed that any unilateral decision to allow the march would be 'a mistake'. The RUC and the Northern Ireland Office said they would announce their decision two or three days before the march.

The march went ahead on Sunday 6 July and all hell broke loose. The rioting began on Sunday and finally came to an end on Friday 11.

By 9 July, according to an RUC report, 60 RUC officers and 56 civilians had been injured while 117 people had been arrested. There had been 815 attacks on the security forces, 1,506 petrol bombs thrown and 402 hijackings. The RUC had fired 2,500 plastic bullets.

The last IRA action took place on 12 July, when an improvised mortar round fell 40 yards short of the RUC/British Army base at Newtownhamilton, South Armagh. Arsonists attacked an Orange hall in Warrenpoint, County Down and another in Rasharkin, County Antrim.

The violence died down on 10 July when the Orange Order decided unilaterally to re-route six parades. The following day, Orangemen and residents agreed to waive another march in Newtownbutler, County Fermanagh and other towns. The Order's gesture was unheard of in its 202-year history. This was the last time the Order marched the Garvaghy Road in Portadown.

In a parallel development, on 9 July the British government assured Sinn Féin that in the event of a new IRA ceasefire, representatives of that party would be allowed to meet with government ministers. A week later, Gerry Adams and Martin McGuinness called for a renewal of the IRA's 1994 ceasefire. The IRA announced the restoration of the ceasefire on 19 July.

THE FINAL CHAPTER

CHAPTER 29

Lara was exhausted. The trouble in Ireland meant she was averaging four hours sleep a night, not quite the eight hours she preferred. She had been working with Mo Mowlam, Secretary of State Northern Ireland, to try to avert a disaster resulting from the Orange Order March in July.

She wasn't over optimistic but was determined to try. It was Friday afternoon and she hadn't been home to Westmoreland Manor for over a month, electing to stay in her South Kensington townhouse so she would be close to her office at Westminster.

One of the benefits of being a Minister of the Crown was having a Government motor vehicle and driver. She began her journey at 5 pm arriving at Westmoreland at 6.30 pm just in time for dinner, with her old friend Lisbeth Forsyth. The two women trusted each other implicitly; no subject was taboo.

Over dinner Lara briefed her confidant about the problems she faced in Northern Ireland. Although sympathetic, Lisbeth couldn't offer anything but her ear.

After dinner, they took their wine into the newly-created theatre room settling into the comfortable seats and watched *Good Will Hunting*.

Next morning Lara loaded her golf clubs into her car and drove to Oak Manor Golf Course. Lisbeth didn't join her as she suffered from osteoarthritis, which prevented her from playing.

Lara played four-ball best ball with Judith Osborne as her playing partner. They didn't win the competition but enjoyed their round nevertheless. Lara was looking forward to riding her horse, Rosie. It had been too long since they rode the Westmoreland grounds together.

Lara was required to be accompanied by two plainclothes policemen, for obvious security reasons. Both were excellent horsemen and had been riding with her for some time. Their names were Senior Sergeant Whittle and Senior Sergeant Westgarth, also known as David and John.

Jason Bryant saddled up Rosie and the other horses. He was the eldest son of Peter, the stable master when Lara was just a young girl.

'Hello Jason. Are we ready to go?'

'Yes, Ma'am. All three are champing at the bit. It should be a good ride.'

'Did you put my new saddle on Rosie?'

'Yes, Ma'am, and a fine saddle it is.'

'It should be. It cost me dearly in the purse. Kings Saddlers made it bespoke.'

'Well, you can't get better than Kings.'

The three riders mounted their horses. The two policemen took their normal positions, one in the lead and one following up the rear.

Lara decided they would take the riverside trail, the same route she took as a girl when her best friend Megan was killed in an unfortunate accident.

It was a leisurely ride as there was nowhere to canter until they reached the moors.

The morning was crisp and clear. The birds were singing and every now and again they could spot a trout catching an insect – it really was a wonderful break from her duties as a Minister of the Crown.

Then, a huge explosion shattered the peace.

Lara and her horse could no longer be seen. The two policemen survived the blast only suffering ruptured eardrums. Only bits and pieces of Lara and Rosie could be identified, spread over the site of the explosion.

Word had got back to Billy Wright that the IRA whore had been blasted to hell where she belonged.

'We got the fucking bitch. Everybody will think it was an IRA hit. Had all the hallmarks of an IRA bomb. If this doesn't fuck up the peace accord I don't know what will.'

Billy and his band of thugs, the Loyalist Volunteer Force, a.k.a. LVF was a small but effective group with tentacles spreading far and wide.

One of their sympathisers was a saddle maker at Kings Saddlery. When he saw the order for Lara de Neville he notified Billy Wright. A plan was hatched whereby the saddle would be stuffed with plastic explosives in addition to wool.

LVF operative Michael O'Meara would stalk the riders from the other side of the river, hidden by bracken and bushes. At the appropriate time, he would set the device off by remote control.

The plan to disrupt the peace treaty failed.

In the early hours of Good Friday, the Ulster Unionist team was still unhappy with some of the detail, particularly the sections dealing with the decommissioning of paramilitary weapons and the release of paramilitary prisoners. A personal assurance from Tony Blair to UUP leader David Trimble smoothed these last ripples of discontent.

At 5.30pm on Friday 10 April 1998, George Mitchell stated: 'I am pleased to announce that the two governments and the political parties in Northern Ireland have reached agreement'.

Lara de Neville's life was taken in a cowardly and cruel way. She had dedicated her life to help others.

She left her fortune, £150,000,000 to various charities in Great Britain and America. She instructed her executor not to use her name on any buildings, either hospitals, or universities that were constructed with the money she bequeathed. She remained humble to the end.

RIP LARA

THE END

Eighth Greater Sin: Usurping the Property ...

"The Astor Orphan": Rich little poor girl – ...

Timeline of the Hippie Movement

The Flowering of the Hippies – The Atlantic

Skinny Dipping in Reality: The Great Hipp...

Erowid Experience Vaults: LSD (also Acid, ...

Janis Joplin – Wikipedia, the free encyclop...

Janis Joplin Friends – Kozmic Blues

World War One Remembered

The Monterey Pop Festival reaches its clim...

Monterey Pop (1968) – IMDb

Monterey Pop (1968) – The Criterion Colle...

Amazon.com: Monterey Pop (The Criterio...

Amazon.com: Buying Choices: Monterey P...

(1) Pinterest: discover and save creative id...

My Vietnam Stories: Chapter 1: Drafted – ...

Google Answers: Military draft lottery

There Was No Rules At All: Stories from Vi...

My War – Army Medic George Banda | Hist...

7 August 1967: George Harrison visits Hai...

Ultimate Summer Road Trip: San Francisc...

Rhinoplasty (Augmentation)

Battle of Hamburger Hill – Wikipedia, the ...

Vietnam War: Battle of Hamburger Hill

Military Amateur Radio System | Veteran S...

1970s Timeline – History Timeline of the ...

List of terrorist incidents in Great Britain –...

Could PM ever be PM? – Telegraph Blogs

Role and work of the House of Lords – UK...

Differences between the House of Lords a...

House of Lords – Wikipedia, the free ency...

Quintin Hogg, Baron Hailsham of St Maryl...

Profumo affair | British political scandal | ...

My first year in the House of Lords | Politi...

1974 in the United Kingdom – Wikipedia, ...

List of terrorist incidents in Great Britain –...

House of Lords – Constitution Committee ...

The Troubles – Wikipedia, the free encycl...

United Ireland – Wikipedia, the free encycl...

Hermes – Shop on the official Hermes on–...

United Ireland – Wikipedia, the free encycl...

Premiership of Margaret Thatcher – Wikip...

Copyright

PHOTOGRAPHS SOUL SURVIVOR

Christine Keeler	Lewis Morley
Monterey Pop Festival-Various Photos	Elaine Mayes
Janis Joplin in Porsche	Emily Chan
Grateful Dead- Cnr. Haight and Ashbury	Herb Green
Human Be In Photos	Luis Ben
Scott McKenzie	GAB